WILLIAM

SHAKESPEARE'S

THE MERRY RISE OF
SKYWALKER

STAR WARS

PART THE NINTH

WILLIAM SHAKESPEARE'S

THE **MERRY RISE** OF **SKYWALKER**

STAR WARS
PART THE NINTH

By Ian Doescher

INSPIRED BY THE WORK OF LUCASFILM
AND WILLIAM SHAKESPEARE

QUIRK BOOKS
PHILADELPHIA

Library of Congress Cataloging in Publication Number: 2020905204

ISBN: 978-1-68369-189-1

Printed in the United States of America
Typeset in Sabon

Text by Ian Doescher
Cover design by Ryan Hayes
Illustrations by Nicolas Delort
Production management by John J. McGurk

Quirk Books
215 Church Street
Philadelphia, PA 19106
quirkbooks.com

10 9 8 7 6 5 4 3 2 1

TO JEFF AND CARYL CRESWELL,

SECOND PARENTS—

THE ANAKIN AND PADMÉ

TO MY HAN—

YET FAR MORE PRESENT,

LOVING, AND ALIVE

DRAMATIS PERSONAE

CHORUS

GENERAL LEIA ORGANA, *of the Resistance*
REY, *a Jedi of the Resistance*
POE DAMERON, *a General of the Resistance*
FINN, *a General of the Resistance*
CHEWBACCA, *a Wookiee of the Resistance*
BB-8, *Poe's droid*
C-3PO, *a protocol droid*
R2-D2, *his companion*
D-O, *an anxious droid*
MAZ KANATA, *of Takodana*
LANDO OF CALRISSIAN, *former General of the Rebellion*
GHOST OF LUKE SKYWALKER, *a Jedi Master*
GHOST OF HAN SOLO, *a scoundrel*
VOICES OF YODA, OBI-WAN KENOBI, ANAKIN SKYWALKER,
    MACE WINDU, QUI-GON JINN, AAYLA SECURA, AHSOKA TANO,
    KANAN JARRUS, LUMINARA UNDULI, *and* ADI GALLIA, *Jedi*
ROSE TICO, *an engineer of the Resistance*
COMMANDER D'ACY, LIEUTENANT CONNIX, KLAUD, SNAP
    WEXLEY, BEAUMONT KIN, AFTAB ACKBAR, NIEN NUNB,
    NIMI, *and* WEDGE ANTILLES, *others of the Resistance*
BOOLIO, *an Ovissian ally of the Resistance*
KALO'NE, *Lando's friend*
ZORII BLISS *and* BABU FRICK, *of the Kijimi Spice Runners*
WICKET *and* POMMET, *Ewoks*
KYLO REN, *Supreme Leader of the First Order*
GENERAL HUX, *of the First Order*
ALLEGIANT GENERAL PRYDE, GENERAL PARNADEE,
    GENERAL QUINN, *and* ADMIRAL GRISS, *of the First Order*

AKI-AKI, PORGS, ORBAKS, KIJIMI SPICE RUNNERS, KNIGHTS OF
REN, FIRST ORDER OFFICERS AND STORMTROOPERS, RESISTANCE
SOLDIERS AND PILOTS, DROIDS, WORKERS, *and* VARIOUS CREATURES

PROLOGUE.

Space.

Enter CHORUS.

CHORUS   Zounds! Menacing, the dead begin to speak!
Heard through the galaxy, though yet unseen,
Comes threat of harsh revenge in voice most bleak—
The sinister, dark Emp'ror Palpatine.
Our General Organa sends a chain   5
Of spies to seek out news past ev'ry border,
Whilst Rey, of Jedi hopes the last, doth train
For battle gainst the devilish First Order.
Their Supreme Leader Kylo Ren is sour,
For he this phantom emperor would see,   10
To conquer any threat to his vast pow'r.
Behold the end of our nonology!
In time so long ago begins our play,
In Force-touch'd galaxy far, far away.

                                                [Exit.

ACT I

SCENE 1.

On Mustafar and Exegol.

Enter KYLO REN.

KYLO   Two rivals, both alike in dignity,
Among the planets, where we lay our scene—
Yet only one shall rule the galaxy.
Unto my solo voice of potency,
A voice was added—bygone Palpatine: 5
Two rivals, both alike in dignity.
Whate'er his purpose, he shall bend to me.
His bold revival cometh unforeseen,
Yet only one shall rule the galaxy.
And Rey, the young, prodigious Jedi she,   10
Hath talent like to mine, though she is green—
Two rivals, both alike in dignity.
The day will come when she shall bend the knee,
When we will reign in peace and might serene—
Yet only one shall rule the galaxy.   15
On both sides I am press'd most ardently,
But in my triumph none may intervene.
Two rivals, both alike in dignity—
Yet only one shall rule the galaxy.

Enter STORMTROOPERS *and several* FOES *of the First Order.*
KYLO REN *slays his foes until he is surrounded by the dead.*

TROOPER 1   Your quest is punctuated by the dead.   20
Success in your endeavor, sir, is all.
KYLO   Thou art dismiss'd, thou and the legion whole.

[Exeunt stormtroopers, bearing away the foes.
If Palpatine shall hide beneath a shroud,
Be sure I'll seek him out where'er he lies.
Upon an errand urgent and profound   25
Have I come hither, pillaging for this:
The Sith wayfinder that leads me to him.
                    [Kylo Ren uncovers a Sith wayfinder
                            and grasps it in his hand.
Darth Vader's former home on Mustafar—
The castle where my grandfather held sway—
Became the final resting place for this   30
Wayfinder that shall lead me to the Sith.
O, pyramid with knowledge long obscur'd,
Show me, I pray, the path that I must take.
                    [Kylo Ren boards his TIE whisper,
                        plugs the wayfinder in, and travels
                            to Exegol, planet of the Sith.
My destiny herein awaiteth me,
Where all is done, or else I am undone.   35
Behold, this giant and forbidding hold,
A building of a most astounding girth.
The dark side of the Force I feel, as though
I were submerg'd beneath the ocean deep
And power dark were water all around.   40
White lightning crackles, flashes, dances quick,
A gloomy symbol of the threat within.
I shall not be deterr'd from purpose true.
Come, lightsaber, and lead me through the dark.
                    [He disembarks on Exegol and walks
                        onto a platform, which descends into a
                            cavern past statues of former Sith.

Although mine enemy awaiteth here,   45
'Tis truly said his lair doth strike my soul.
These tow'ring statues of departed Sith
Would chill the bravest heart and toucheth mine.
Still, Kylo Ren shall not be shaken, nay—
Whilst I have life, I shall not be sent hence.   50

        Enter EMPEROR PALPATINE, *hidden.*

PALPATINE   At last, young Kylo Ren, thou hither com'st.
        Snoke train'd thee well, 'tis certain.

KYLO   —Yet Snoke died
        By this, my hand, and thou shalt follow him.

PALPATINE   My dearest boy, Snoke was a thing I made—
        A valuable creation of the Sith,   55
        With still more of his like available.

    KYLO REN *walks past a tank of liquid holding many*
    bodies that resemble Supreme Leader Snoke. Enter
    several SITH ACOLYTES, *working on the tank.*

I have been ev'ry voice thou ever heard'st:
When I do speak, 'tis in the voice of Snoke
Or, when I wish, 'tis in Darth Vader's voice—
Inside thy head, these voices echo round,   60
And I control the strings that move their mouths.
'Twas always I who led and guided thee
And now have brought thee here, my will to serve.
Thy vain First Order was an overture,
Preamble to profounder music still—   65
A mere beginning to my pure design.

Forsooth, I'll proffer thee a greater gift.

KYLO   Thou shalt die first—thine aspirations, too.

PALPATINE   I died before, yet death retains me not—
              The underworld is no match for the Sith.   70
              The dark side of the Force unveils a path,
              The road less travel'd by, which openeth
              A world of wondrous, new abilities
              That some consider most unnatural.

                          [Palpatine comes forward, connected
                            to an Ommin harness. Kylo Ren points
                                his lightsaber toward Palpatine.

KYLO   Yet what couldst thou—unnatural, indeed—   75
              Give me that I do not have?

PALPATINE   —Ev'rything.
              Behold my broken, chipp'd, and weaken'd hands,
              And see therein the possibilities.
              An Empire new shall from these ashes rise.
              Around us even now my fleet doth rise—   80
              Grim Star Destroyers waiting rank on rank,
              In numbers such as none could comprehend.
              This have I plann'd these many slumb'ring years.
              Whilst some men dream, I have been at my work
              Assembling this: the army thou shalt lead.   85
              The Final Order's might shall ready be,
              And all is thine if thou dost what I ask—
              Kill thou the girl, the Jedi line conclude.
              Become, then, what thy grandfather could not—
              Darth Vader: powerful, yet not enow.   90
              Thou shalt rule o'er the galaxy entire,
              The newfound Emperor who takes my place.
              Beware, though—she is not whom thou believ'st.

KYLO	Who is she? Tell me all that thou dost know,
	And down this pathway gladly shall I go.	95

[*Exeunt.*

SCENE 2.

Inside the Millennium Falcon.

Enter FINN, POE DAMERON, *and* CHEWBACCA,
seated at the holochess board.

CHEWBAC.	[*aside:*] Egh, auugh![1]
POE	—What thinkest thou, then,
	Wookiee? Shalt
	Thou play, or ever gaze upon the board?
	Thou hast kept eyes on the phenomenon—
	Puff'd, paus'd, waddl'd about, and grunted so—
	Yet when wilt thou advance and take thy move?	5
FINN	The furball cannot beat us ev'ry time.
POE	And yet he doth. The startling fact is now
	Almost admitted universally.
FINN	How doth he so? For 'tis unknown to me.
POE	This gentleman with hairy coat of brown?	10
	In such a game, wherein the pieces have
	Bizarre and diff'rent motions, various
	And variable values, one may oft
	Mistake what's but complex for what's profound.
	Attention is call'd powerf'ly to play,	15

---

[1] *Editor's translation:* Should I stare at the pieces long enow,
Mayhap I can arrange them diff'rently.

And if thou pay'st attention, thou shalt see:
He cheateth, it is plain.

CHEWBAC.   —Auugh![2]

POE   —Nay, I jest!
Thou art two hundred fifty years of age—
With many years in foreign travel spent—
'Tis natural thou art superior.   20

FINN   Forever and a day thou takest for
Thine ev'ry move, which is wherefore we think
Thou cheatest. Faster play, and we shall none.

                         [A sensor beeps.

CHEWBAC.   Egh, egh, auugh![3]

FINN   —Fear thou not, we'll nothing touch.

POE   We shall not turn the game off, by my troth,   25
Yet we may get a very thrilling bit
Of superstition from this fit of thine.

              [Chewbacca walks to another part of the ship.

FINN   Forsooth, the beast is cheating.

POE   —Verily.
His agitation, represented here,
Is so excessive that this officer   30
Hath not the slightest doubt of Chewie's guilt.

              [Poe turns the holochess board off.
                 Finn and Poe follow Chewbacca.

---

[2] *Editor's translation:* Nay, if thou call'st me cheater, we are through!
      I have pull'd arms off stronger men than thou.
[3] *Editor's translation:* I must unto the cockpit presently.
      Touch not the game, unless ye would be touch'd—
      My sure and certain victory is nigh.

Enter KLAUD, *working on the ship.*
Enter R2-D2 *aside, near the top hatch.*

           Good Klaud, I hope thou fix'd the power surge,
           Else shall the *Falcon* grounded be, I fear.

KLAUD   Reeyah, reeyah.
                      [Poe sits in the cockpit with Chewbacca.

POE   —Good Chewie, let us hie—
           Our quick approach we make, to meet the one   35
           Who bringeth critical intelligence.
           'Tis the desire of all parties concern'd
           To keep our bold affair from public view—
           At least for this, the present time, until
           We've further opportunity to make   40
           Investigation—lest a garbl'd or
           Exaggerated story maketh way,
           Misrepresented, to society.
           T-minus five and we are there, my friends!
                      [Finn approaches the top hatch.

FINN   Artoo, holla. Stand'st thou prepar'd for this?   45
           Thy swift assistance I may yet require.

R2-D2   Meep, squeak! *[Aside:]* Born ready was I, here to serve!

The Millennium Falcon *flies inside an icy base and positions*
itself beneath an ice processing structure. FINN *opens the top*
hatch. Enter BOOLIO *in an opposite hatch, facing him.*

FINN   Ah, Boolio! 'Tis fine to see thee here.
           Bring'st thou aught for us? Prithee, say thou dost!

BOOLIO   A newfound ally is my gift to you: 50
           A clever spy from the First Order's ranks

Who would assist ye in your ev'ry scheme.

FINN   A spy? Thy words are music for mine ears—
Who is this praiseworthy and fearless soul?

BOOLIO   Nay, I know not. Take thou this message, Finn,   55
And transfer it to Leia presently.
Make haste, for the First Order follows on!

>   *[Boolio lowers a drive to Finn via a cable.*
>   *Finn inserts the drive into R2-D2.*

R2-D2   Beep whistle whistle hoo, meep squeak beep meep?

FINN   This may be most significant, Artoo.
Fill thou thy databanks with knowledge, quick!   60

>   *[The data on the drive begins*
>   *to transfer to R2-D2.*

R2-D2   Squeak whistle hoo!

Enter a legion of TIE FIGHTER PILOTS *in their*
ships, approaching the Millennium Falcon.

TIE PILOT 1   —My target lockèd is.

POE   Finn, work with speed! Or else we are the goose,
Cook'd for the filling of First Order plates.
They come with flash of fire most terrible,
Accompanied by densest cloud of smoke   65
And noise to naught but thunder comp'rable!

FINN   'Tis nearly finish'd.

>   *[The data transfer concludes.*

R2-D2   —Whee!

FINN   —Ho, now fulfill'd!

>   *[Finn unplugs the drive as*
>   *Boolio begins to lift it.*

How can we thank thee for this, Boolio?

	Thyself thou hast endanger'd for our cause!
BOOLIO	Win ye this war, and all is reconcil'd—
	Your victory is recompense enow.

> *[Exit Boolio. Finn closes the top hatch,*
> *then sits at a turret gun. The* Millennium
> Falcon *flies away from the pursuing TIE*
> *fighters. Poe knocks the ship into a wall.*

CHEWBAC.	Auugh, egh![4]
POE	—Alas, I know! Apologies!
	It must admitted be that thou hast some
	Good reason for thy doubt. My fault excuse.
FINN	[*aside:*] Once more I take my seat to fire on foes!
POE	Finn, wherefore shoot'st thou not these ships? Hath all
	Thine ordinary manner vanishèd,
	Thine ordinary occupations been
	Neglected or forgotten? Shoot, I pray!

> *[Finn shoots at a TIE fighter and destroys it.*

FINN	A-ha! The first is done, with more to come.
POE	How many yet remain? I do confess,
	True, dreadf'ly nervous I had been and am!
FINN	In troth, too many for my comfort, Poe.
CHEWBAC.	Auugh![5]
POE	—Thought most wondrous, Chewie, well devis'd!
	O, this great problem is, at length, Finn, solv'd:
	Let us put boulders in the path of TIEs.
FINN	'Twas foremost in my thoughts as well. Aim, guns!

Line numbers: 70, 75, 80, 85

---

4 *Editor's translation:* If thou dost wreck my ship, I'll wreck thy pate!
5 *Editor's translation:* Behold the bridge toward which we approach—
   Could it become a weapon in our hands?

         [Finn shoots at a support structure, which
         collapses after the Falcon *flies under*
         it and destroys two TIE fighters.

A fair maneuver. Fly, then, to our base!

POE   More fighters make approach—a mighty wave

And we a tiny vessel on the sea.   90

[*Aside:*] When first this apparition I beheld—

For scarcely I regard these foes as less—

My wonder and my terror were extreme.

[*To Chewbacca:*] How thick, brave Chewie, is this ice
                             wall?

CHEWBAC.   —Auugh![6]

         [The Millennium Falcon *bursts through a*
        wall of ice into space. It jumps into lightspeed
        and is pursued by many TIE fighters.

POE   This either shall be brilliant or be mad—   95

Th'idea of it hath ne'er occur'd to us.

FINN   What is this lunacy? Fie on it, Poe!

POE   'Tis lightspeed skipping, gambit hazardous,

True wretchedness, indeed, woe ultimate!

I'll jump through lightspeed quickly, then again,   100

Repeating once and twice and thrice and more,

Until the stratagem hath shaken all

These foes who would destroy us as we flee.

FINN   When didst thou learn such fearful, horrid tricks?

         [As the Falcon *jumps through*
        lightspeed, more TIE fighters smash
        into obstacles and are destroyed.

---

[6] *Editor's translation:* Art thou insane? Heard'st not my warning, Poe?
    Thy schemes are nearly ludicrous as Han's!

CHEWBAC.   Egh, egh![7]
POE   —'Tis well Rey is not here. Tut, tut!   105

> *After the next lightspeed jump, enter a* GIANT BEAST,
> *opening its mouth to swallow the* Millennium Falcon.

    This is our final shot, belike fore'er!
    I plan to fan this spark into a flame,
    Which may yet prove a blaze of glory, friends.
    This bold idea upon my fancy seiz'd;
    I lost myself forthwith in reverie.   110
    Hold tight, courageous comrades, for we fly
    And death or triumph cometh, by and by!
>   *[The* Falcon *shoots past the beast. Exeunt*
>   *Poe Dameron, Finn, Chewbacca, Klaud, and*
>   *R2-D2 in the* Millennium Falcon. *The final TIE*
>   *fighters are devoured by the beast. Exeunt.*

SCENE 3.

On Ajan Kloss.

Enter REY.

REY   The training which I once began with Luke
    Here on the planet Ajan Kloss persists.
    I spend my days in Leia's tutelage,

---

[7] *Editor's translation:* Rey would be most unhappy, were she here!
  Thou takest far too many chances with
  This ship, which is most dear to her and me.

So that I may a stronger Jedi be.
She hath the knowledge and th'experience   5
To teach me ev'ry lesson I need know.
Once I had no one, liv'd a lonesome life,
Reclaiming wreckage back on dour Jakku,
Yet longing to be known, accepted, lov'd.
How shaken was my life when, suddenly,   10
A kindly, wand'ring droid came unto me.
Then follow'd one who fled the trooper life.
He led me to a Wookiee and a rogue—
These all became the dearest friends to me.
Hook'd by a greater cause—Resistance—I   15
Escap'd my former home and came to see
Undream'd-of planets, stars, and forms of life,
Now open to this sometime scavenger.
I sought Luke Skywalker in his exile,
Vied with his stubbornness, that he might come   20
Erase our fear with Jedi might. But he
Refus'd to help us—so it seem'd, until
Surprisingly he did appear on Crait,
Establishing his legend for all time,
Bewitching Kylo Ren so we could flee.   25
Embolden'd, the Resistance liveth on;
Great General Organa leadeth us,
Undaunted by our disadvantages.
It is to her, to hallow'd ancestors,
Luke, all the Jedi now one with the Force—   30
E'en these I bid: be with me, be with me.
Distressingly, I sense they're not with me.

Enter GENERAL LEIA ORGANA *and* BB-8, *approaching* REY.

LEIA   Be patient, Rey, their voices shall yet speak.

REY   My thoughts turn pessimistic, and methinks
          It is impossible to hear their words—   35
          The voices of the Jedi gone before.

LEIA   Naught is impossible. Speak thou the words.

REY   Naught is impossible. Thus shall I strive
          To know and to believe. Excuse me now,
          The training course awaits my daily run.   40
          Perchance 'twill free my mind for clearer thought.

LEIA   Take thou Luke's lightsaber, and all my hopes.
               [Exit General Leia Organa as Rey begins to run.

REY   The training doth begin, a simple trot.
          My legs go coursing through the trees and fog,
          Atop the rocky face, past waterfalls,   45
          Unto a chasm o'er a craggy drop.
          My helmet here awaiteth, which I don
          As flieth the remote toward the spot.
                              [A remote flies into view as
                                   Rey puts on her helmet.
          Down, blast shield, to remove mine outer sight,
          That I mine instincts must rely upon.   50
          Now, balancing atop the sturdy rope,
          O'er the abyss I parry, block, and dodge!
          Past this wide gulf, I leap to climb a tree
          And cut a single length of scarlet cord—
          My mark that half the course is now complete.   55
          I clasp it in my hand and make return—
          Fleet-footed like my life depended on't—
          And hurdle o'er the prior opening.

Enter KYLO REN *above, on balcony,*
holding the mask of DARTH VADER.

KYLO   With newfound knowledge of the girl, e'en Rey,
         Reported to me by the Emperor,   60
         Our earlier connection I'll restore
         That she and I communication share.
         O, mask once worn by my grandfather strong,
         Grant me the pow'r to find her once again.
                                          [Rey trips.

REY   How many times have I this course fulfill'd,   65
         And never did my feet slip errantly.
         I sense some presence here, which I've not felt
         Since last I was too close to Kylo Ren.
                          [The remote begins shocking her.
         Alas, the small remote appears to have
         A mind its own, as if it were controll'd   70
         By human bidding rather than machine.
         Now grows mine anger suddenly—I'll slash
         And kill the impish, rotten flying pest
         Sans thought of anything around me here!
                      [She slashes wildly with her lightsaber,
                                destroying many trees.
         If my lightsaber shall not do the deed,   75
         I shall be more creative in my wrath!
                  [Using the Force, she picks up a stick and
                      spears the remote to a tree with it.

KYLO   I feel her fury, burning with the heat
         Of sun that rises o'er a desert plain.

REY   Now I do sense it! Ren is in my head,
         And in a flash such horrid images   80

Rush like a torrent into my mind's eye.
My parents taken rapidly from me,
My darker self install'd upon a throne,
The hand of Kylo Ren held out to me
In solemn invitation and desire,   85
The face of Luke, my master, sad and scar'd,
The voice of Han ere slain by his own son.

KYLO   Her visions are mine own, as if we two
Shar'd but one eye, one ear, one mind, one hcart.
I must needs find her and discover more.   90

                                    [Exit Kylo Ren.

BB-8   Blic blooblis roohblik bleezooz roilzoon blip!
                        [Rey looks at BB-8, who has been
                              caught under a felled tree.

REY   Poor BB-8, profound apologies!

            She frees him and they return to the Resistance
                base. Enter GENERAL LEIA ORGANA.

            I finish'd not the training course today—
            Distractions plentiful took focus hence.
            I do not feel myself—be patient, pray,   95
            I know it seemeth I excuses make.

LEIA   Seems, Rey? Nay, say what is; I know not seems.
REY   Belike I am exhausted, nothing more.

                Enter LIEUTENANT CONNIX.

CONNIX   Good General, the *Falcon* is not back
            And our commander seeketh your advice.   100
                    [Rey hands Luke's lightsaber back to Leia.

REY   One day I shall obtain the inner worth
             To wield the saber of thy brother Luke—
             When I have earn'd it, fain would I receive't.
BB-8   Rooqzoom bluu zzwablav blayzooz flliblik rooh
             Zoon bleezilf roilflig blip?
REY   —Nay, BB-8,   105
             Thou mayst not help me earn it, kindly droid.
LEIA   Nay, never underestimate a droid.
REY   Yea, master.

                    Enter NIMI.

NIMI   —Ho, the *Falcon* hath return'd!

Enter POE DAMERON, FINN, CHEWBACCA, R2-D2, *and* KLAUD
in the Millennium Falcon, *which is in flames. Enter* C-3PO *and*
various RESISTANCE PILOTS *and* SOLDIERS, *including* MAZ KANATA,
ROSE TICO, SNAP WEXLEY, AFTAB ACKBAR, *and* BEAUMONT KIN.

POE   Anon, the ship! Look to the ship, I pray!
             The rear, it is aflame. The front as well!   110
             The lurid luster of a fire that I
             Cannot force my imagination to
             Regard as yet unreal. Attend to it!
REY   Holla, Poe. What is this I hear of spies?
POE   To all appearance, we have—by thee, Rey—   115
             Been temporarily abandonèd.
             We could have us'd thy help.
REY   —How went your task?
POE   But poorly, truth be told. No pestilence
             Hath ever been so hideous to me.

REY   Han's ship in tatters maketh its return—   120

POE   [*seeing BB-8:*] The thousand injuries that I have seen
           I've borne as best I could, but when upon
           My droid they venture, I shall vow revenge.
           I prithee, speak: what didst thou to the droid?

REY   What didst thou to the *Falcon*? Wilt thou say,   125
           Or art thou too embarrass'd to respond?

POE   The *Falcon* is in better shape than he.
           No word speaks the deliverer, I see.

REY   Nay, little BB-8 is not afire.

POE   What parts of him remain are not afire.   130
           My nerves are very much affected, Rey.

REY   Pray, speak thou plainly, tell me what hath happ'd.

POE   Speak thou! The buzz of curiosity
           Doth overwhelm my patience and my tongue.

REY   There is a word created for such men   135
           As thou art, Poe; wouldst thou hear me declare't?

POE   What is't? Expressions piquant would I learn.

REY   Thou art most difficult, as though thou wert
           A door with many locks but none of keys.

POE   And thou art—O, it is beyond mine art   140
           Of speech to speak the words. I candidly
           Confess my feelings are e'en now of the
           Most singular, myster'ous character—
           Incomprehensible, perplexing, too!

                                        [*Finn approaches.*

REY   Finn, friend forever—safely thou return'st!   145

                                   [*Rey and Finn embrace.*

FINN   Yet barely, if the truth be known.

REY   —Foul moods
           Do overwhelm the senses, is it true?

FINN	Foh, mean'st me?
REY	—Him.
FINN	—Forever and a day.
REY	Is there a spy?

                                           [Chewbacca approaches.

CHEWBAC.	—Auugh![8]
REY	[*to Poe:*] —Thou didst lightspeed skip?
POE	Indeed I did, our safety to secure.
	The consequence is clear: we did return.
	All this was scarcely more than justice, troth.
REY	Yet, Poe, thou knowest the compressor's weak.

150

---

[8] *Editor's translation:* This folly-fallen pilot would assault
The *Falcon* by his lightspeed skipping. Fie!

POE   I know it well; 'twas I who present was,
             Unlike thyself. Thou look'st to number one,   155
             We're number two and must look to ourselves.

FINN   [aside:] These two shall ever be like fighting kin.

REY   Thou canst not make the *Falcon* lightspeed skip!

POE   The evidence runs contrary to speech,
             For truly, thus did I. It hath been driv'n   160
             To an extremity, 'tis clear to all.

FINN   We have but landed these few moments past—
             I bid ye, friends, can we not find some peace?

REY   What happen'd?

POE   —More bad news, and nothing more.
             Such as will happen now and then.

REY   —No spy?   165

POE   To all this I am sorry I cannot
             Reply with anything but this: no, spy!

REY   Thou frightest ev'ry word from its right sense!
             Speak plainly: made we contact with a spy?

FINN   A message we receiv'd from th'inner ranks   170
             Of the First Order, yet near not escap'd.

BB-8   Zood flirflit blee flew blayzoom zoodreej flir
             Bluu bloozilf blip bleeblip blav bleeblik zood
             Blox zzwaflig flitrooh flirblip bleereej blee
             Zoom bluuzilf bliprooq blooblay zoon blic zoom   175
             Rooq blayzooz bliprooh zzwaflli flit fligblee.

POE   My strict integrity comes into play:
             Thou dropp'dst a tree upon him? Is this true?

REY   Thou blewest both subalternators, Poe?

POE   Belike thou shouldst have been with us, if thou   180
             Art so concernèd o'er the *Falcon*'s fate.
             Remarkable! Though this plain word is but

	A feeble term t'express my meaning full.
REY	Well knowest thou I would be—
POE	—Yet art not.

Make up thy mind to be annoy'd at me: 185
Remain'st thou here to train, but to what end?
Of all our fighters, talent hast thou most.
We need thee there, not here. Soft—I have done.
[Poe walks aside with others.

FINN	The man speaks fervently but truly, Rey.
REY	What is the message ye glean'd from the spy? 190
POE	My friends and soldiers both, pray take ye heed.

[All gather around Poe.

We have th'intelligence giv'n by the spy
Decoded, that we may its secrets know.
Perhaps no exhibition of the kind
Hath e'er elicited so general   195
Attention as this ominous report.
The worst hath been confirm'd: somehow, some way,
The Emperor, e'en Palpatine, return'd.

LEIA	[*aside:*] Base name of evil creeping from the past!
ROSE	Wait, is this foul report believable? 200
	Shall we assume this spy hath truth declar'd?
AFTAB	It cannot be! The Emperor is dead!
	He fell within the last war with a zap.
BEAUMONT	Dark science, cloning, such dread physic as
	Was only known of by the wretchèd Sith. 205
POE	Look down into th'abysmal distances—
	It doth appear he long hath plann'd revenge,
	And now his followers build something vast
	That hath seen many years' development:
	A fleet such as the galaxy ne'er knew. 210

'Tis call'd the Final Order. Sixteen hours
Have we until attacks begin upon
Each world that currently doth freedom know.

CHEWBAC.   Egh, auugh![9]

POE   —The Emperor, his fleet—they hide
Within the provinces unknown, a world   215
Call'd Exegol. This is, indeed, no dream.

R2-D2   Beep, meep, squeak!

C-3PO   —Exegol doth not appear
On any star chart. Legend knows it as
The hidden planet of the wicked Sith.

                         [*Rey runs to find a book.*

REY   [*aside:*] To find the Sith—of such I late have read.   220
'Twas Master Luke did first pursue the task.

POE   Yea, Palpatine abided all this time,
And pull'd the strings of evil's puppetry.
The heart had ceas'd to beat—volition, though,
Had not departed from his awful mind.   225

LEIA   Concealèd in the shadows from the start.

MAZ   If we would stop him, we must find him first.
The furtive Exegol we must detect.

                       [*Rey returns with the book.*

REY   Pray, General, a word.

LEIA   —Friends, give us leave
To speak a word or two.

             [*Exeunt all, talking among themselves,*
                       except Rey and Leia.

REY   —I know how we   230
May find myster'ous Exegol.

---

[9] *Editor's translation:* 'Tis ever thus! Shall there ne'er rise a peace?

LEIA	—Pray tell!
REY	Luke was in search of it for many years

LEIA   —Pray tell!

REY   Luke was in search of it for many years
    And nearly found it, too, ere he expir'd.
    This book—among the sacred Jedi texts—
    Containeth ciphers far beyond my ken.   235
    To get to Exegol, one needeth this:
    A Sith wayfinder, which a compass is
    That leadeth swiftly unto Exegol.
    Thus shall we stop what we both know shall come—
    'Tis right that I conclude what Luke began: 240
    Find Exegol and find the Emperor.

LEIA   Nay.

REY   —Sans thy blessing I'd not go, but will.

Indeed, I shall. 'Tis e'en what thou wouldst do.

Enter POE DAMERON, FINN, CHEWBACCA, C-3PO, *and* BB-8.

POE   The ship hath been repair'd and may depart,
             To face a terror for which there's no name.   245

REY   Thou hadst it right before, Poe, I must go.
             I'll venture forth to follow in Luke's path
             And seek out Exegol. I shall begin
             Where first Luke's trail turn'd cold, the desert lands
             Forbidden of Pasaana.

POE   —Yea, I know.   250
             There is a game of puzzles, which is play'd
             Upon a map. We shall go with thee, Rey.
             [*To Chewbacca:*] Pray Chewie, hast thou the compressor
                                                         fix'd?

CHEWBAC.   Egh.[10]

REY   [*to Finn:*] —This I'd do alone.

FINN   —Alone with friends.
             Bid us not leave thee; we are not afeard.   255

REY   'Tis far too dangerous.

FINN   —We fly as one.
             Together gone, together safe and well.

CHEWBAC.   Auugh, egh![11]

BB-8   —Flig fllireej zoonblis zood blay blee
             Zooz bleezilf zood!

C-3PO   —I heartily agree!

---

[10] *Editor's translation:* All is prepar'd. We may depart anon.
[11] *Editor's translation:* They call me stubborn, yet thou, Rey, art worse.
    Let not thy pate be thick—we all shall go.

REY   How can I question, with such friends as ye?   260

                              Enter ROSE TICO.

FINN   Rose, 'tis thy chance to seek thy fate and come.
ROSE   The General hath ask'd me to remain
             And study all the intricacies of
             The Star Destroyers of the past, that we
             May stop the fleet if ye discover it.   265
FINN   Nay, spak'st thou *if*?
ROSE   —When.
FINN   —Yea, say *when*, forsooth.
                                        [Exit Rose Tico.
POE   [*to Rey:*] We must depart or we shall be too late
             And turn'd out of our office by the time.
             Thy mien, it darkens. What doth plague thy thoughts?
REY   Naught. Simply a goodbye I yet must say.   270
                              [C-3PO approaches R2-D2.
C-3PO   Should it befall that I do not return,
             I would thou knewest what a friend thou art,
             And ever wert, to me. My best, in troth.
R2-D2   Beep, whistle, squeak! [*Aside:*] O, golden droid—with
                                                            whom
             I long have squabbl'd, gladly did annoy—   275
             Shall thou, now, in this parting moment make
             Me shed a droidly tear in friendship's name?
             Companion loyal, ever by my side,
             Thou art the better half who makes me whole.
                              [Rey approaches Leia.
REY   Much would I say to thee ere I take leave.   280
LEIA   Tell me when thou returnest; gladly would

I see thee then and hear thy pressing words.
                          [Leia hands Rey Luke's lightsaber.
Thou worthy art, hast earn'd it many times.
                                      [They embrace.
Rey, never be afeard of who thou art.
                          [Rey, Poe, Finn, Chewbacca,
                          C-3PO, and BB-8 board the
                          Millennium Falcon. *Exeunt others.*

CHEWBAC.   Auugh![12]
REY   —Yea. I would not from this team depart.   285
                                      [Exeunt.

SCENE 4.

On Kylo Ren's command ship,
the Steadfast.

Enter KYLO REN.

KYLO   My mask, which once by Snoke's ire I did crush,
            Hath been repair'd, forg'd solid once again.
            A master craftsman, Albrekh, did the deed,
            Employing ancient forges of the Sith.
            Sarrassian iron holds the pieces fast,   5
            And the result is that the helmet is—
            Like mine own skill and mine abilities—
            E'en stronger than it previously was.

---

[12] *Editor's translation:* 'Tis well to venture forth with thee again—
Our band complete, an escapade at hand.

Enter KNIGHTS OF REN *and various* STORMTROOPERS.
Enter GENERAL HUX, ALLEGIANT GENERAL PRYDE,
GENERAL PARNADEE, GENERAL QUINN, *and other*
OFFICERS *of the First Order. All are seated.*

TROOPER 1   [*aside, to Trooper 2:*] The Knights of Ren.
TROOPER 2   [*aside, to Trooper 1:*]   —A horrid
                                        sight, by heav'n!
             [*Kylo Ren throws Boolio's head on the table.*

KYLO   We have a spy conceal'd within our ranks—   10
            A base and spineless rogue, who hath convey'd
            A treas'nous message to th'Resistance vile.
            Whoe'er this traitor be, they'll not stop us.
            With what I did espy on Exegol,
            The great First Order quickly shall become   15
            An empire true, with all the pow'r to match.
            Good Gen'ral Hux, I sense a deep unease
            About how I appear before thine eyes.
                             [*All turn and look at Hux.*

HUX   Thy mask? Nay, verily. Well done, dread sir.
PARNADEE   It suits thee well. Thine aspect it improves.   20
QUINN   Forgive me, sir, I fain would speak my mind:
            These allies new on Exegol—is't not
            A cult deriv'd from some foul madman's schemes?
            We need no conjurers and soothsayers.

PRYDE   They conjur'd Star Destroyers by the score.   25
            If this be cultish, I shall gladly join.
            The Sith fleet shall increase our resources
            Ten thousand fold. If magic 'tis, 'tis well.
            Such range and pow'r correct the errant gaffe
            That was Starkiller Base and all its flaws.   30

PARNADEE   We must increase recruitment mightily.
             The pastures of the galaxy are ripe,
             And we shall harvest all the young we need.
QUINN   This fleet—doth it come to us as a gift?
             A present freely proffer'd, nothing more?   35
             Or shall the giver turn to asker soon—
             What doth the Emperor require of us?
             What treasures shall he ask for in return—
                     [Using the Force, Kylo Ren begins choking
                      General Quinn and raises him to the ceiling.
KYLO   Prepare to conquer any worlds that dare
             Defy our might. My knights and I shall fly,   40
             Bring back the scavenger and watch her die!
                                                        [Exeunt.

SCENE 5.
On Pasaana.

Enter Rey, Poe Dameron, Finn, Chewbacca, C-3PO, *and* BB-8.

POE   A desert world with sunlight burning bright,
             Resembling bleak Jakku or Tatooine—
             Too much of sand and dryness for my taste,
             Despite the tranquil, somewhat magical
             Strange radiance that hovers over all.   5
             C-3PO, art certain 'tis the place?
C-3PO   Indeed. These are th'exact coordinates
             That Master Luke hath left behind for us.

Enter Aki-Aki, *dancing and celebrating.*

POE   What is this gathering we happen on?
              There is no quiet here, nor silence, nay.   10

C-3PO   The Aki-Aki Festival of the
              Dear Ancestors, methinks! This jubilee
              Occureth only once each forty-two
              Years—an auspicious number, verily.

FINN   'Tis fortunate.

C-3PO   —Forsooth, it truly is!   15
              This festival is widely known both for
              Its kites most colorful and also sweets
              Delectable beyond imagining.
                              [Rey, Poe, Finn, and Chewbacca
                                    turn and stare at C-3PO.

              [Aside:] Alas, 'twas never my intention to
              Become the center of attention here.   20
              Perchance they stare at something at the rear?
                              [C-3PO turns and looks behind him.

REY   I ne'er have seen a festival like this,
              Such heartfelt celebration, full of life!

FINN   I ne'er have seen so few wayfinders, troth.

POE   There e'er are chance First Order–led patrols   25
              At such events and in enormous crowds.
              No day elapses, but it brings news of
              Decease of some acquaintance at their hands.
              Keep heads down—yea, Chewbacca, thou as well,
              Although thou art far taller than the rest.   30
                      [Chewbacca bends down to keep his head low.
              Let us part company, that we may see
              Whatever local knowledge may be found.
                              [All walk in different directions.

REY   [aside:] The colors, dancing, joy on ev'ry face.

Behold these groups of children, seated whilst
A show of puppetry amuseth them!   35
They laugh withal their bellies, heartily
Enjoying what the elders have display'd.
Such innocence, such wonder, and such bliss—
Did I e'er know such happiness as this?

Enter an Aki-Aki named NAMBI GHIMA.
She approaches REY, *and* C-3PO *translates.*

NAMBI   Mayedo-bu!
C-3PO   —She sayeth welcome here.   40
NAMBI   Meyay de la bonotui. Kobu
             Dig gamba danni beez. Bodidi oo
             Di Nambi Ghima.
                              [Nambi Ghima places a necklace
                                   around Rey's neck.
C-3PO   —She is Nambi Ghima.
REY   A name most excellent and beautiful.
             I am call'd Rey.
NAMBI   —Giodo lobuto?   45
C-3PO   She would be honorèd to learn the name
             Of thine ancestral family as well.
REY   I have no fam'ly name. I'm call'd plain Rey,
             And bonny Rey and sometimes Rey the curst.
             [*Aside:*] Alack, most suddenly my senses shriek—   50
             'Tis Kylo Ren! The fiend doth contact me
             Through our most strange and enigmatic bond.

She walks aside. Enter KYLO REN *aside, in his chamber.*
They are joined in the Force and see each other.

KYLO   The Emperor, e'en Palpatine, would see
            Thee dead.

REY   —Thou foundest a new master, yea?

KYLO   Nay, I have plans of which he knoweth naught.   55
            My hand in partnership I offer'd once
            To thee, and sens'd thou wish'dst to take it up,
            To share the mantle of my power vast.
            Yet wherefore didst thou not?

REY   —Thou hadst the chance
            To kill me and did not. Why didst thou not?   60

KYLO   Thou canst not hide fore'er, Rey, not from me.
            We two are like a planet and its sun,
            Each circling round the other evermore.

REY   I spy betwixt the cracks of thy black mask
            And see the haunted man who lies therein.   65
            Thine eyes shall never cease to see the deed
            Thou didst inflict upon thy father kind—
            The death of good Han Solo, whom thou kill'dst.

KYLO   Dost thou still count the days that have elaps'd
            Since thy two parents left thee on Jakku?   70
            Such pain I feel within thee, pulsing like
            A perilous volcano soon t'erupt.
            Such anger, too, which powereth the blast.
            I would not kill thee, Rey. Yet I shall find
            Thee, turn thee to the dark side of the Force.   75
            When once again I proffer thee my hand,
            I'll warrant thou shalt take it gratefully.

REY   Thus shall we see if ever we two meet.

                       [Kylo reaches out and grasps the
                     necklace around Rey's neck, pulling
                         it off her. Exit Kylo Ren.

        [*Aside*:] Our close connection turns to something more—
        He hath th'ability to touch me here,   80
        To be where I am momentarily
        That what is mine is his and his is mine.
                        [*Rey runs to find Poe and Finn.*
        [*To Poe and Finn*:] We must depart unto the *Falcon*,
                              now.

FINN   Yet wherefore must we so, Rey? Canst thou tell?

REY   'Tis Ren. He shall arrive anon, I fear.   85

Enter KYLO REN, ALLEGIANT GENERAL PRYDE, *and a*
FIRST ORDER OFFICER *holding the necklace, above on balcony.*

OFFICER 1   We had the necklace analyzèd, sir.
            'Tis clearly from the system Midian—
            Pasaana, the Forbidden Valley there.

KYLO   Prepare my ship, alert the local troops.
            Send forth a new division presently.   90

PRYDE   E'en as thou sayest, Supreme Leader Ren.
                    [*Exeunt Kylo Ren, Allegiant*
                    General Pryde, and Officer 1.

Enter STORMTROOPER 3, *pointing a gun toward* REY, POE
DAMERON, FINN, CHEWBACCA, C-3PO, *and* BB-8, *below.*

TROOPER 3   Be still, or I shall use my gun on ye!
            [*Into radio*:] The fugitives of the Resistance have
            I found—all units hie ye hither quick—
                    [*An arrow strikes Stormtrooper 3*
                      in the helmet, and he dies.

Enter LANDO OF CALRISSIAN, *in a mask.*

LANDO   I bid ye, follow. I shall keep you safe.   95
                    [Rey, Poe, Finn, Chewbacca, C-3PO, and
                    BB-8 follow Lando into his treadable.

                    Enter KALO'NE, *in the treadable.*

                    Kind Leia sent a message unto me.
                    [To Kalo'ne:] Nadiyya tobiah.
KALO'NE   —Okay!
                                        [Kalo'ne starts driving the treadable
                                        away from the crowd.
FINN   —My friend,
                    How didst thou find us?
LANDO   *[taking off his mask:]* —Wookiees in a crowd
                    Have their partic'lar way of standing out.
                                        [Chewbacca embraces Lando.
CHEWBAC.   Auugh![13]
LANDO   —Yea, 'tis well to see thee, too, my friend.   100
C-3PO   This man is Gen'ral Lando of Calriss—
REY   We all know who he is, C-3PO—
                    His fame doth, like a herald, ere him go.
FINN   Forsooth, it is an honor, General.
POE   Brave General, we have come here upon   105
                    A search for Exegol, a secret that
                    Doth not permit itself to be reveal'd.
LANDO   'Tis plain, and I know what it is ye seek.

---

[13] *Editor's translation:* Brave Lando, holla! Thou art most well met,
    Companion of our bygone glory days.

          [He pushes a button, revealing a
                 hologram of a Sith wayfinder.

But two were made, which maketh them most rare.

REY   The Sith wayfinder. Luke Skywalker hath   110
Come hither to find one of them.

LANDO   —I know,
For I was with him on the venture grand.
We two were trailing a most horrid beast—
A Jedi hunter, Ochi of Bestoon.
'Twas said he had a clue that leadeth to   115
A Sith wayfinder. Flew we halfway cross
The galaxy to find him here at last.

             Yet when we found his ship, abandon'd 'twas—
             With neither clue nor wayfinder for us.

REY   Is Ochi's ship upon the planet still?   120

LANDO   'Tis in the desert, where he left it once.

REY   We must unto the ship and search again.

                                 [The sound of TIE fighters is
                                       heard in the distance.

LANDO   Hark! By mine ears, your time is running out.
             I have a feeling bad about this sound.
             Ye shall find Ochi's ship in yonder land,   125
             Beyond Lurch Canyon. Go, and be ye swift!

POE   All gratitude, good General. Thy zeal
             To serve a friend is most commendable.

CHEWBAC. Egh, egh.[14]

LANDO   —And I as well, dear Chewie.

REY   —Pray,
             A word ere we depart. Our Leia needs   130
             Skill'd pilots in the fight gainst tyranny.

LANDO   My days of flying ships past stars and space
             Have long since pass'd, yet do me one small thing:
             Give Leia all my love when thou seest her.

REY   'Twould better be if thou gav'st it thyself.   135
             Farewell, and thank thee greatly for thy help.

                       [Rey, Poe, Finn, Chewbacca, C-3PO, and
                            BB-8 disembark from the treadable.

LANDO   *[aside:]* Such words play on me unexpectedly,
             My conscience prick'd as when a bee doth sting—
             Retirement, mayhap, is no life for me.

---

[14] *Editor's translation:* Would that we had more time to reconnect.
   Long have I wish'd to see thee, treasur'd friend.

[Exeunt Lando and Kalo'ne in the treadable.

POE   There! To the skimmers let us swiftly run.   140
           I shall secure a pair that we may use.
           Th'excitement 'mongst the masqueraders is
           Prodigious and may keep us from their sight.
                    [They run toward the skimmers, C-3PO
                         trailing slightly behind the others.
                         Poe begins hot-wiring one of the vehicles.

FINN   How is such mischief in thy skill set, Poe?

C-3PO   Ye need not worry, I am here at last.   145
           You must have been most worried over me!
                         [Many Aki-Aki see what Poe is
                              doing and begin yelling.

POE   Just as if they had all been reading mine
           Own thoughts, they notice and make their approach!
           We must get hence, or else we are undone!
                    [Poe, Finn, and C-3PO board one skimmer.
                         Rey, Chewbacca, and BB-8 board the
                         other. They fly away. Exeunt Aki-Aki.

           Enter STORMTROOPERS.

TROOPER 4 The fugitives are in our sight at last,   150
           And we shall make pursuit with utmost speed.
                    [Four stormtroopers begin chasing them,
                         two troopers each on two treadspeeders.

REY   They fire on us, and ably we respond—
           Trade shot for shot and fear no consequence!
                    [The treadspeeders' repulsor lifts fire,
                         shooting one stormtrooper from each speeder
                         into the air, flying after the skimmers.

C-3PO   Foh, they fly now!
FINN   —They fly now?
POE   —They fly now!
             How terrible a spectacle, by heav'n—   155
             What dangerous peculiarity!
             We shall split up and make them chase us still.
REY   Such bold maneuvers shall keep them away.
                        [Poe flies his skimmer into a ravine.
POE   A blessèd thing 'twould be for spirits if
             We leave the rogues astern. Are they yet gone?   160
FINN   So doth it seem, for they are not behind.
C-3PO   Most excellently done, Sir Poe, in faith!
                        [One stormtrooper treadspeeder
                                    catches up to them.
             Most terribly 'twas done, Sir Poe, in faith!
BB-8   [to Rey:] Blic flliblik roohblis zzwa flew blavroil blee
             Reej zzwarooq bliprooh roilflig zzwa fllizoon!   165
REY   Nay, BB-8, 'tis not the time for pranks!
BB-8   Zilf flewblox zzwaflib flitreej blic zoomrooh.
                        [BB-8 sparks a tank on the skimmer, sending
                            it flying into the air. It explodes, sending
                                yellow powder everywhere. Trooper 5
                                    flies through the cloud of powder.
TROOPER 5   Alack, this powder flieth fore mine eyes,
             And I am, for the moment, blind as—ah!
                        [Trooper 5 runs his treadspeeder into a rock. He
                            is ejected from his seat, and Rey shoots him.
REY   The words of Leia proven in a trice—   170
             Nay, never underestimate a droid!
FINN   We are pursued by this determin'd fiend!
             The fast and noisome speeder that he drives

Must have a weakness I shall find out yet.
A-ha! Here is a rope, which, if thrown straight   175
Around the tread, may stop the wretched foe.
                    [Finn throws the rope, which winds itself
                              quickly around the treadspeeder.
Poe, twist the skimmer—send him for a ride!
                    [Poe quickly turns the skimmer aside,
                         causing the stormtrooper and his
                              treadspeeder to hurl into a rock.

POE   The hopes of our humanity fulfill'd!
FINN   Hurrah! Now let us swiftly to our friends.
REY   There, in the distance—I spy Ochi's ship!   180
              What is this vision, dancing on my sight
              And calling forth forgotten memories?
              This ship—'tis certain I have seen't before,
              Unless 'tis some deception of my mind.
                              [Poe's skimmer approaches Rey's.
POE   Rey, come thou close. All thou and I have got   185
              To do is pack it up, turn to, and then—
                    [The final stormtrooper shoots the skimmers,
                         sending Rey, Poe, Finn, Chewbacca,
                         C-3PO, and BB-8 plunging through the air.
                              They land on a sinkhole of dark sand.

REY   We shall not be outdone by one of them!
CHEWBAC.   Auugh![15]
                    [They all shoot at the stormtrooper, who
                         is hit and explodes against the side of a
                         mountain. All begin to sink in the sand.
POE   —What is this, some rough-hewn, hell-born jest?

---

[15] *Editor's translation:* Destroy the knave. Yea, let him taste our wrath!

A desolation but surrounded by
Another desolation, verily!   190

BB-8   Zooz zzwablay roilblox zzwaflew blic blav blik,
          Bluu flliflit blis flir fllirooq zoon blip blik!

REY   Take hold of something fixèd fast and firm!

C-3PO   O, agony beyond comparison!
                              [Poe exits through the trapdoor,
                                        followed by BB-8.

FINN   Rey, hear me: I ne'er spake the words to thee—   195
                              [Finn, Chewbacca, and C-3PO
                                    exeunt through the trapdoor.

REY   Alas, what is the poor Resistance's chance
          When e'en the ground doth look at us askance?
                              [Exit Rey through the trapdoor.

ACT II

SCENE 1.

On Ajan Kloss.

Enter GENERAL LEIA ORGANA, ROSE TICO, *and* SNAP WEXLEY.

SNAP	Wise General, reports are reaching us
	Of raiding at th'ancestral festival.
LEIA	This mission is our ev'rything and all—
	We cannot fail. Hast any word from Rey?
SNAP	The *Falcon*, sadly, unresponsive is. 5
ROSE	Must thou speak such foul words in somber tones?
SNAP	How was't I spake?
LEIA	—Grant me one favor, Snap,
	Which shall be giving me a needed boon:
	Speak thou with optimism, if thou canst.
SNAP	Yea, ma'am. All is terrific, by my troth— 10
	Ne'er shall your eyes believe how all turns out!
	We shall have victory, and that sans doubt!

[Exeunt.

SCENE 2.

On Pasaana.

Enter POE DAMERON *and* BB-8 *in a cave below the sinking fields.*

POE	Step altogether indescribable,
	Which led to sharp fall! Rey, Finn, where are ye?

Enter C-3PO.

C-3PO   Thou call'dst not my name, sir, yet I am safe.

                    Enter REY.

POE   I have been frantic with each species of
               Profound and wild excitement. Art thou well?   5
REY   Indeed, yet where is Finn?
POE   —Or Chewie, too?
               Near an emporium of furs is he!

                  Enter CHEWBACCA *and* FINN.

CHEWBAC.   Auugh![16]
FINN   —I am present, safely here withal.
C-3PO   Ah, Master Finn. Our company's complete.
POE   What is this place, with darkness all imbued?   10
               Out are the lights—out all! A cavern grim.
C-3PO   'Tis not the afterlife, is it? Are droids
               Allow'd herein?
POE   —Methought our cause was lost.
               'Twould be the fostering of folly if
               We had but perish'd neath the sinking sands.   15
C-3PO   It may yet be.
FINN   —Which way to exit, friends?
                          [Rey lights her lightsaber. Poe turns on his
                              flashlight, whose glow is far weaker.
POE   [*aside:*] My light is unto hers as is a worm—
               Whose tail doth light a fraction of the night—

---

[16] *Editor's translation:* Of all th'adventure I have ever known,
    Ne'er hath the ground itself sunk neath my feet.

	Compar'd unto the brightest sun e'er seen.	
	It doth give me distinct conception of	20
	The marvels my friend hath accomplishèd.	
REY	We must make haste. [*To Finn:*] What was it thou	
	wouldst say?	
FINN	I follow not—what do thy words denote?	
REY	When we were sinking in the dodgy sand,	
	Thou saidest, "I ne'er spake the words to thee—"	25
FINN	In faith, I later shall reprise the theme.	
POE	Fell those few simple sounds within mine ear,	
	And what would be the consequence? Why wait?	
	Perhaps when Poe is gone, then wilt thou tell?	
FINN	Perchance 'twill be a better time, forsooth.	30
POE	We shall within a burrow made of sand	
	Greet death in all its dark and fearsome robes—	
	A simile of sorrow and defeat—	
	And still our secrets clutch unto our chests?	
FINN	I shall unfold my confidences once	35
	Thou tell'st us of thine underhanded past—	
	How thou canst hot-wire vehicles so fast,	
	For instance.	
POE	[*aside:*] —Change the subject swiftly, Poe!	
	[*Aloud:*] I would not know what hath these tunnels	
	made—	
	I dread whatever curse we have invok'd.	40
	[*They begin searching the caves.*	
C-3PO	To judge by the circumf'rence, it appears—	
POE	Think'st thou my words themselves have little or	
	No meaning? Droid, hast thou not heard me speak?	
	I said I would not know, and there's an end.	
	What is this here?	

FINN	—A speeder thou hast found. 45
REY	'Tis old, methinks.
C-3PO	—Perhaps the driver we
	Shall find herein.
BB-8	—Flib blayzilf blee roohflit
	Zoom roil bloo flliroooq blikblis bleebluu roil
	Flew blayzooz zoodblic blee flig zzwareej zood.
POE	Yea, BB-8, I heartily agree. 50
	'Tis most unlikely one could e'er survive
	Th'oppressive closeness of the atmosphere.
C-3PO	Behold, a hex charm, common symbol of
	Sith loyalists!
REY	—Sith?
FINN	—If 'twas Ochi's, then—
REY	Luke sens'd it—Ochi never left this place. 55
FINN	His final resting place was in this cave.
POE	He did pursue his ship, yet reach'd it not.
	True—desperate, but scarcely desp'rate more
	Than we. Belike the fate we fac'd was his.
FINN	How, then, did Ochi reach the surface?
REY	—Nay, 60
	He did not, for observe his cold remains.
FINN	Fie on it—thou hast spoke the words aright.
POE	Bones—horrid sight! I like not bones. My mind
	Endeavors to reply, and yet my tongue
	Refuseth its own office suddenly. 65
C-3PO	A set of bones glad tidings never doth
	Suggest.
BB-8	—Blikroil zoom bloozoon bloorooq blik!
REY	I see it, BB-8. Well spotted, droid!

       [BB-8 blows upon the sand, revealing
         a buried dagger. Rey picks it up.

    [Aside:] The evil in this blade is evident—
    Deeds horrible hath it accomplishèd.   70
    It is some portent of a darkness great.

POE   Look at the writing, etch'd into the blade.
    What are these secrets most artistical?

C-3PO   I shall attempt to translate what's thereon.
          [C-3PO looks at the blade.

    The hid location of the wayfinder   75
    Hath been inscrib'd upon this dagger sharp.
    'Tis certainly the clue that Master Luke
    Long searchèd for.

POE   —What doth it say? Do tell!
    That is, if it would be agreeable
    Unto thy protocol and etiquette!   80

FINN   How may we find our way to th'wayfinder?

C-3PO   Alas, I may not tell you. Pray, forgive.

POE   Thou speakest languages twenty point three
    Fazillion, yet thou canst not translate it?
    Thou must have talents more than one or two. 85

C-3PO   I read it plain as any schoolchild's text,
    And know precisely where th'wayfinder is.
    Unfortunately, 'tis composèd in
    The runic language of the wicked Sith.

REY   What import makes thou importune us so? 90
    What doth the language matter, Threepio?

C-3PO   My programming forbids me to divulge
    Its meaning, yea, or translate what it says.

POE   The one time we would beckon thee to speak
    Thou canst not do so, and thou callest it 95

A matter of unpossibility?

C-3PO   I am unable, sir. Apologies.
               Mechanic'ly incapable am I
               Of speaking a translation from the Sith.
               The legal rule was by the senate pass'd—   100

Enter a VEXIS SERPENT *behind* C-3PO.

BB-8   Blee blisflit zoonflig zzwablav blikroil blee!
C-3PO   A serpent, foul and nasty—O, alack!
               I prithee, save me from the dreadful beast!
                         [Poe points his blaster at the vexis.
REY   Nay, Poe, stand down. Methinks 'twill turn out well.
                         [She hands her lightsaber to Finn
                              and steps toward the vexis.
               [Aside, to the vexis:] Peace, friend, we have not come to
                                   do thee harm. 105
               I see thou hast been injur'd mightily,
               The pain of which must plague thee. Be thou still,
               For I believe I have the pow'r to help.
                              [The snake bristles.
POE   I'll shoot it. 'Twill be executed to
               The best of my ability, in sooth.   110
FINN   Nay, be thou sure of Rey—she knows herself.
                         [Rey puts her hand on the vexis's
                              injury, using the Force to transfer life
                              to it. The wound slowly heals.
VEXIS   *[aside, to Rey:]* Particular and radi'nt sense—e'en life
               Thou offer'st! Now, go upward, exeunt.
                         [Exit vexis snake, swiping the wall with its
                              body and creating a hole out of the cave.

BB-8	Blay flewzooz rooh blox zzwablav flit flirzood
	Rooq flliblip zood zoonblis zoomflit roil flit 115
	Blikrooh reej blooflig bluuzilf zood blic bloo?
REY	I transferr'd to the snake a bit of life—
	Force energy from me to him dispens'd.
BB-8	Zilf zoodroil fllirooq zoodroil flliblip flit
	Zoom roohblox bluuflib flirblik flit?
REY	—Methinks 120
	Thou wouldst have done the selfsame, BB-8.

> [*Chewbacca puts the dagger in his belt.*
> *All walk outside toward Ochi's ship.*

Enter the KNIGHTS OF REN *and* STORMTROOPERS, *aside.*

C-3PO	We cannot fly within this ancient ship.
POE	We must proceed, until we someone find

	Who can the dagger translate—e'en, perhaps,	
	A helpful droid, and not one of thine ilk.	125
	Marry, this is all that could be desir'd.	
C-3PO	To the *Millen'um Falcon* let's return.	
POE	With all thy cogs this mystery explore:	
	They shall wait at the *Falcon*, us to take.	
FINN	Belike to fling us in the pits of Griq.	130
POE	And use thee as a simple target droid.	
	'Tis hardly possible to e'en conceive	
	Th'extremity of terror thou wouldst have.	
C-3PO	Ye both make points most excellent. At times.	

          [Rey stares into the distance.

REY	[*aside:*] A feeling doth wash o'er me like a flood.	135
	Some ripple in the Force—the darkness comes.	
FINN	What is it, Rey? What art thou feeling? Speak.	
REY	I shall be close behind ye. All is well.	

     [She hands her staff to Finn and descends
       toward the open plain while the others
        climb to Ochi's ship and enter it.

POE	Let us discern what help the ship can give—	
	Fire thou the old converters speedily,	140
	Search narrowly the lines, controls, and gears!	
C-3PO	A filthy ship, if e'er I one beheld.	

        [Poe flips switches, and the
          ship's controls light up.

POE	No dirge will I upraise, for all bodes well:	
	There is still life within the old ship yet!	
FINN	Yet where is Rey, and wherefore takes so long?	145
POE	Finn, help me, prithee. O, be with me still.	
FINN	Chewbacca, hie outside and find thou Rey—	
	Tell her we must soon fly or be seiz'd.	

CHEWBAC.   —Egh![17]
                    [Chewbacca runs out of the ship toward
                        Rey. The Knights of Ren approach
                            him and take him prisoner.

POE   I cannot speak or think for worrying—
                 What is she doing? Why doth she delay?   150

FINN   'Tis Ren, I fear, or she would tarry not.
                     [Finn goes out of the ship and sees
                      Chewbacca being put into a transport by
                      the Knights of Ren. Exeunt Chewbacca, the
                        Knights of Ren, and stormtroopers. Rey,
                        aside, takes position in the plain below.

        Enter KYLO REN in his TIE whisper, flying toward REY.

REY   [aside:] Anon he cometh, even Kylo Ren—
                 Now have I put my friends in jeopardy.
                 Did I not wish to take this trip alone,
                 Instead of placing them in peril, too?   155
                 Nay, say not so, Rey—'tis unjust of thee.
                 I would not have it other than it is,
                 To have my friends and comrades with me here.
                 Instinctively, lightsaber by my side,
                 Next shall I face the threat that Ren presents. 160
                 Once did I fear him, thought he was too strong,
                 Lack'd I the confidence to face his might.
                 Opposing him by impulse natural,
                 Negated I his efforts when he would
                 Gaze on the hidden secrets of my mind.   165

---

[17] *Editor's translation:* I shall at once, e'en as thou sayest, Finn.

E'en then I did resist, and have done since—
Resistance hath become my strength and stay.
Put now each small distraction from thy mind,
Let full serenity be in thy soul.
Advance he shall, and ready shall I be.   170
Yea, long have I imaginèd this scene:
The moment when our conflict would resume.
He comes at me with ship at racing speed,
Endeavoring to fill my mind with dread—
Perchance he shall be shock'd, discovering   175
A Jedi utterly prepar'd for him,
Who neither shirks nor cowers at his name.
Ne'er was an instant critical as this!

      [Rey flips above Ren's ship as it approaches.
      She slices off one of its wings, and it crashes
      loudly. A transport flies into the sky.

FINN   Rey, look! The fiends hath taken Chewie hence!

REY   'Tis more than rocks—this transport is immense.   180
      Yet if I do believe, I'll make it still.

      [Rey extends her hand, using the Force
      to halt the transport. Kylo Ren emerges
      from the wreckage of his ship.

POE   [*aside:*] What strange abilities thou hast, rare lass!
      I feel thee now—I feel thee in thy strength.
      Thou art a Jedi true and masterful.

KYLO   [*aside:*] Her powers are immense, yet mine prevail.   185

      [He extends his hand, using the
      Force to pull the transport, too.

REY   [*aside:*] A test of wills, yet mine shall greater prove!
      Each second I have train'd, I train'd for this!

KYLO   [*aside:*] She shall not overcome me—never, nay!

REY   [*aside:*] The villain's strength shall not o'ertake mine
                                                            own!
                    [*Lightning emerges from Rey's hand and
                        strikes the transport, which explodes.*
           Nay, Chewie! Foh, what have I done? Nay, nay!   190
FINN   Alack, for Chewie sake, ne'er let it be!
KYLO   [*aside:*] This o'erabundance of the Force doth shock—
           Ne'er did I think she had such stuff in her.
                                            [*Exit Kylo Ren.*
POE   We must away! They come! TIE fighters come!
FINN   Come, Rey, or we are finish'd! Get thee gone!   195
                    [*Finn and Rey run back to Ochi's ship.*
REY   [*aside:*] Chewbacca, friend and furry confidant,
           Forgive me for this o'eruse of my will,
           The loss of life that cometh by my hand.
           Belike I never would have sought to train
           As Jedi, were the consequences thus.   200
                    [*Rey, Poe, Finn, C-3PO, and BB-8 take off in
                        Ochi's ship. Exeunt Poe, C-3PO, and BB-8.*
           [*To Finn:*] I lost control.
FINN   —'Twas not thy fault, though,
                                                            Rey.
REY   'Twas, truly.
FINN   —Nay, 'twas Ren who forc'd thy hand—
REY   Our Chewie's gone, and words bring him not back.
           The power that destroy'd him came from me.
           Finn, there is much thou dost not, couldst not, know.   205
FINN   Fill thou the gaps within my knowledge, Rey.
REY   A vision came to me, a portent bleak—
           The dark throne of the Sith I gaz'd upon,
           And there was seated—

FINN   —Ren, so fathom I.

REY   Both Ren and I were seated there, we two,   210
Together, reigning o'er the galaxy.
And thus, this vision full of tragedy
Wills me to leave my base vocation, flee,
And free my comrades from calamity.

                                  [Exeunt.

SCENE 3.

Aboard the Steadfast.

Enter GENERAL HUX *and* ALLEGIANT GENERAL PRYDE.

HUX   The scavenger's junk ship, as *Falcon* known,
We have recover'd, though she slipp'd our bonds.
Commanded by the errant Knights of Ren,
Much loss we've suffer'd, most regrettably.
A transport was destroy'd—

PRYDE   —Yea, the report   5
Was clear in ev'ry detail. Is there more?
Or hast thou merely come to lay the blame?

HUX   One item more, Allegiant General:
Another transport to the desert flew,
Which captur'd an important prisoner.   10

PRYDE   A prisoner? Pray, bring it hither.

Enter CHEWBACCA, *bound and led by* STORMTROOPERS.

CHEWBAC.   —Egh![18]
HUX   The beast once flew withal Han Solo.
CHEWBAC.   —Auugh!
             Egh, egh, auugh, auugh![19]
PRYDE   —Let it be taken hence,
             Unto the room interrogation six.
             Let us awhile employ collective wit   15
             To think how we may make best use of it.
                                                        [Exeunt.

SCENE 4.

Aboard Ochi's ship, the Bestoon Legacy, *and on Kijimi.*

Enter REY, POE DAMERON, FINN, C-3PO, *and*
BB-8. *Enter* D-O, *unmoving, aside.*

POE   Eight hours remain until the mighty fleet
             By th'Emperor may be sent harshly forth,
             Which shall the skies turn ashen—sober, too.
             What shall we do?
FINN   —What choice hath fate giv'n us?
             We must flee back unto our base posthaste.   5
POE   Was it not fate—whose name is also sorrow—
             That led us here? No time have we to flee.
             We shall not, must not give up. If we do,

---

[18] *Editor's translation:* Ye villains, I shall have your blood for this!
[19] *Editor's translation:* Let not his famous name escape thy lips,
     Thou who unworthy art, past ev'ry sense.
     Would I were free of bonds, in twain I'd tear
     Thee, ripping limb from limb and bone from bone!

Then Chewie died for naught and we are lost.

FINN The dagger was to Chewie fasten'd tight. 10

POE There must, then, be another way—no one
Can e'er dissever this, my soul, from the
Belief we'll make it right.

FINN —We can but find
The wayfinder withal th'inscription set
Upon the knife blade, which is lost to us. 15

C-3PO 'Tis true. Th'inscription liveth only in
My memory.

POE —Trash of all trash! Is't so?
Th'inscription that was on the dagger lies
Within thy memory?

C-3PO —Yea, Master Poe.
Translation from forbidden languages, 20
However, can in no wise be retriev'd.
Unless, that is, one would attempt a full
Redactive mem'ry bypass.

FINN —Full mind what?

C-3PO A dangerous and sinful act perform'd
On witless droids by dregs and ruffians. 25

FINN Let us do thus! Fulfills it ev'ry need!

POE I know of one black market droidsmith, yea.
[*Aside*:] Mute, motionless, aghast, afeard am I,
Though, at the thought of it.

C-3PO —Black market, what?
A droidsmith? Fie!

POE —Upon Kijimi, though— 30
Its turbulency tells a terror tale.

FINN What wrong is found upon Kijimi, Poe?

POE Bad fortune had I on Kijimi once—

It fills my heart of hearts with dread and woe.
Yet, if this mission fails 'tis all for naught,   35
All we have done these many months and years.

FINN   Together strive we, till the final note.
                          [Rey stands and takes Finn's hand.

REY   For Chewie, then, our company goes forth.

POE   This taking of the hands, is this our sign
                  Of spirits moving music'ly as one?   40

FINN   Yea, hold hands fast—let not the moment pass.
                          [Poe takes Finn's other hand.

POE   For Chewie, then, a play of hopes and fears.

C-3PO   [*aside:*] I shall not, from this congress, be forsook.
                          [C-3PO takes Poe's other hand.

POE   Then from our present pathway part not, friends,
                  Unto Kijimi, there to make amends.   45

                  They set course for Kijimi. Enter CHORUS.

CHORUS   The happy few toward Kijimi fly,
                  Believing they escape from ev'ry foe.
                  Yet as their ship departs, I pray, espy
                  A rival ship pursues them as they go.
                          *[Exit Chorus. BB-8 spots D-O, approaches
                             it, and inserts a cable into D-O's head.*

BB-8   Zoom fllizoon blis roil rooh bloo zzwa blikroil   50
                  Blip roilreej flir rooq bleeflig blisbluu blee
                  Zilf flitblav flitzood rooh flewblee blic blee.
                          [D-O awakens.

D-O   Charg'd battery! Holla!

BB-8   —Blox roohflib bloo!
                          [BB-8 and D-O roll to Rey.

D-O	Holla!
REY	—Well met, small droid.
	[She reaches out to touch D-O.
D-O	—No, prithee! Nay!
BB-8	Flig flewblip roohblik zzwazooz flitreej flli 55
	Zoomblis blox flliroil flit?
REY	—It doth appear
	That someone hath abus'd it mightily,
	And made it most afeard of being touch'd.
	[To D-O:] Thou shalt not need to fear me, little one.
	Thou art, herein, among a group of friends, 60
	And thou art welcome to our merry band.
POE	Unto Kijimi make we our approach!
	Take heed, friends: nothing there is motionless—

They all disembark on Kijimi. Enter
STORMTROOPERS *and* RESIDENTS OF KIJIMI.

	The vile First Order searcheth ev'ry street,	
	Ubiquitous and menacing throughout	65
	Kijimi City. This, a place of crime,	
	Is ripe for the First Order's heavy hand.	
	Stay close, I pray; I know what we must do.	
C-3PO	Yea, as do I: we must depart anon!	
POE	Tut, Threepio. Pray, follow, gentles all—	70
	It seemeth death hath rear'd himself a throne	
	In this strange city, lying all alone.	
	Yet still we may succeed. Let us advance—	

Enter ZORII BLISS, *pointing her blaster at* POE'S
head, and other KIJIMI SPICE RUNNERS.

ZORII	'Twas said thou wert at Monk's Gate spotted, though	
	Methought thou wert not dumb enow t'return.	75
POE	Thou wouldst be most surpris'd how dumb I am.	
	I stand beneath the mystic moon, ensnar'd.	
REY	Who is this?	
POE	—Zorii 'tis. Meet Rey and Finn.	
	O, this is but a dream within a dream.	
ZORII	Most gladly would I pull this trigger now.	80
POE	In human memories and tearful lore,	
	I have seen thee do worse—	
ZORII	—Yea, for far less.	
POE	Within this nook most melancholy, there	
	The traveler—e'en I—have met, aghast,	
	Thou, mem'ry of the past. Some discourse do	85

	I beg of thee, to talk ere thou dost shoot.
ZORII	Yet I would see thy brains besmirch the snow.
POE	My soul a stagnant tide was, when I left,
	And certain 'tis thou still some anger hold'st.
	Yet, Zorii, I beseech thee for thy help.
	We must needs crack this golden droid's head ope,
	And that most speedily.
C-3PO	—Beg pardon, sir?
POE	We have come here in search of Babu Frik,
	Who gentlest of all gentle names doth take.
ZORII	Yet Babu only worketh for the crew,
	Which is no longer thou.

90

95

REY   —What crew mean'st thou?

ZORII   'Tis not surprising he ne'er mention'd it—
               Thy friend's employment was in running spice.

FINN   In faith, thou wert spice runner? Is it so?

POE   [aside:] And thus, the words were spoken!
                                   [To Finn:] Yea, wert thou 100
               A stormtrooper?

REY   —Wert thou spice runner, Poe?

POE   Wert thou a scavenger? My soul at least
               A solace hath in knowing we could play
               Fore'er this daft game.

ZORII   —Thou hast not fore'er.
               Still dig I from the hole thou putt'st me in   105
               When thou departedst to Resistance join.
               [To Rey:] Thou, woman, art the one for whom they
                                                        search.
               The bounty for her capture amply shall
               Our coffers fill. Djak'kankah!

POE   —Nay speak thou
               Djak'kankah not, thou pilgrim shadow, pray—   110
                      [Rey moves quickly and disarms Zorii and
                      other members of the gang. Zorii falls, and
                          Rey points her lightsaber at Zorii's face.

REY   We earnestly and badly need thine aid,
               I prithee.

ZORII   —Though thou shalt not care nor heed,
               Methinks thou art a friend and not a foe.

REY   I care more than thou knowest, verily.
               Give me thy hand and let us start again.   115

        [Rey turns off her lightsaber and extends her
        hand, helping Zorii up. They all sneak through
        the streets. Exeunt stormtroopers and residents.

ZORII   The vile First Order bringeth walkers here,
          Stay close and we shall thither make our way!

FINN   *[aside, to Poe:]* Poe Dameron, spice runner! Ha, a fig!

Enter OMA TRES *as all walk into the bar he tends. He shakes*
his head as they walk past and speaks to himself.

OMA   Since I have many years bartended here,
          Time hath put strange events athwart my path,   120
          Sights never seen have pass'd my watchful eyes.
          Here walks—O, heav'n!—a band that seemeth base—
          The metal knave, he rankleth. Out he stays,
          Were my shrewd rules establish'd presently.
          Alas, the central statutes in the bar   125
          Were never set by mine astute decrees.
          Thus shall I let them pass me peacef'ly. O,
          Ne'er shall a creature say that Oma Tres
          Hath ever treated any type with hate,
          Abusèd all the strength his status bears,   130
          And acted aught but kindly ev'ry day.
          Nay, I shall serve sans further statement. O,
          Regardless, they that pass near Oma Tres
          May feel my sneer when walking past the bar,
          May sense the deep chagrin where falls my stare,   135
          May grasp resentments and distaste nearby—
          If I have hurt them, O, then mercy grant.

                                    [Exit Oma.

Enter BABU FRIK *as the others enter his workshop.*

ZORII   Good Babu, thou recall'st Poe Dameron?
               He cameth hither to entreat thy skill—
               To search the mem'ry of this golden droid.   140
                              [*Babu hooks* C-3PO *up to his*
                                        machines with wires.

C-3PO   O, wherefore did I to this plan agree?
               Belike I am malfunctioning herein.

REY   Wise Babu Frik, canst help us with this deed?

BABU   Muh nyoba apaa Babu a bwookin.

REY   Pray, Zorii, canst thou translate what he says?   145
               Think'st thou this plan shall work?

ZORII   —Ediga oo
               M'Babu muh. Ayy toouh nanga booh?

BABU   Nundo mutiga uh nudo nudo!

ZORII   He saith he hath found aught within the droid's
               Forbidden mem'ry banks. It is some words,   150
               Translated from the Sith.

REY   —'Tis what we need.

FINN   He found it, yea!

ZORII   [*to Poe:*]   —Who spend'st thou time withal
               Who speaketh Sith?

POE   —Can he but translate—[*Aside:*] Nay,
               I'll speak to him an unimpassion'd song.
               [*To Babu:*] Canst make him, Babu, translate what it
                                        says? 155

BABU   Nuh oola baba tikta. Eh zahzo.

ZORII   Indeed, yet it requireth a complete—

C-3PO   Complete wipe of my memory, as fear'd.

POE   If he the message translates, then the droid

	Recalls naught? Years of love shall be forgot	160
	Within the workings of a minute? Yea?	
BABU	Wadoh da memory go bleah! Bleb bleb!	
C-3PO	O, woe is me! Is there no other way?	
FINN	Does not fine Artoo back thy mem'ry up?	
C-3PO	My fate I would not trust to such as he—	165
	His storage units are reputed for	
	Their unreliability, in troth!	
REY	Thou know'st the odds far better than we do—	
	Thou quotest them abundantly enow—	
	Have we a choice? Speak true and we shall heed.	170
C-3PO	Yea, if this mission fails 'tis all for naught,	
	All we have done these many months and years.	

                  [C-3PO is silent for a moment.

POE	Thou restest so compos'd, that I behold	
	And fancy thou art dead. Hark, Threepio—	
	Thou hast gone silent, droid. Say, art well?	175
C-3PO	[*aside:*] This moment doth require my sacrifice—	
	No other choice by logic or by odds	
	Is left, if we our purpose would fulfill.	
	I have been helper, translator, and serv'd	
	As best I could to aid my masters kind.	180
	Yet now am I turn'd linchpin in the plot,	
	The very spoke that holds the wheel in place.	
	Upon the instant, I perceive the truth:	
	They are not merely masters, by my troth—	
	They have become my comrades, whom I love	185
	With ev'ry sense that's given to a droid.	
	How fortunate to live the life I've led—	
	Thus shall I give it gladly for my friends.	
	It is the cause, it is the cause, my soul,	

	So go I to't, though all shall be forgot.	190
	[*To Poe:*] Not merely quiet—taking, at the last,	
	A final look at ye, my family.	
D-O	Sad!	

                                                     [A light shines in the window.

ZORII	—Night raids shall begin anon. I shall	
	Outside and keep a lookout for our foes.	
POE	I'll go with thee, to seek for danger in	195
	The jewel'd skies.	
ZORII	—Still thou dost trust me not?	
POE	Dost thou trust me beneath thy burning eye?	
ZORII	Nay, truly.	

                                      [Exeunt Poe Dameron and Zorii Bliss.

| BABU | —Ha! | |

Enter KYLO REN, GENERAL HUX, ALLEGIANT GENERAL PRYDE,
and ADMIRAL GRISS *on balcony, in the command ship.*

KYLO	—Report now, Gen'ral Pryde.	
PRYDE	A new development ariseth, sir.	
	The Knights of Ren have trapp'd the scavenger.	200
GRISS	A settlement known as Kijimi, sir.	
HUX	Shall we destroy the city, thinkest thou?	

                                [Ren holds up a hand to silence Hux.

| KYLO | At once we shall fly thither, with this ship. | |

                         *[Exeunt Kylo Ren, General Hux, Allegiant
                              General Pryde, and Admiral Griss.*

| C-3PO | An idea strikes me of another way— | |

                         *[Babu touches a wire that makes a spark fly
                         from C-3PO's head, and C-3PO goes silent.*

| BABU | Nuhgoo kahka. | |

Enter POE DAMERON *and* ZORII BLISS *on balcony, keeping watch.*

POE   —The searing glory which   205
                   Hath shone hath faded quickly! How long hath
                   Kijimi been so much oppress'd? Dost know?

ZORII   The vile First Order kidnapp'd ev'ry child
                   Some time ago. My soul cannot abide
                   The cries that far too oft I heard betimes.   210
                   I have acquir'd enow that I may leave—
                   Anon unto the colonies I'll fly.

POE   Ah! What is not a dream by day to she
                   Whose eyes are cast on things around her, with
                   A ray turn'd back upon the past? How shalt?   215
                   Is not thine ev'ry pathway block'd to thee?
                              [Zorii pulls a medallion from her pocket.
                   Medallion of First Order captain's rank!
                   Ne'er have I seen a real one in the flesh.

ZORII   Free passage through whate'er blockade exists,
                   The privilege to land on any ship—   220
                   Methinks it is a consummation, Poe,
                   Devoutly to be wish'd. Wouldst come withal?
                              [Zorii pulls back her mask to reveal her eyes.

POE   My heart doth tremble at the beam of thy
                   Soul-searching eyes, yet I cannot retreat
                   From this momentous fight until 'tis done.   225
                   Perchance already 'tis, and we have lost.
                   A call we issued when on Crait we fought,
                   Which none did answer—no one join'd the fray.
                   So fearful are the masses, giving up.

ZORII   I'd not believe that thou believ'st 'tis so.   230
                   The evil forces win when they make thee

Believe thou art alone. Remember? There
Are more of us.
                    [*Exeunt Poe Dameron and Zorii Bliss. In*
                        the workshop, Rey applies oil to D-O.
D-O   —A squeaky wheel have I!
                    [*D-O rolls back and forth with no squeaking.*
My thanks!
REY   [*to Finn:*]   —Aught of this scene doth strike me wrong.
'Tis Ochi's ship—I know where last I saw't.   235
The day my parents left me on Jakku.
They flew away aboard that vessel, Finn.
FINN   For certain?

Enter POE DAMERON *and* ZORII BLISS.

ZORII   —Listen! A Destroyer comes!
POE   We must fly hence or desolately fall.
Have we the needed information, eh?   240
Art done, Babu?
BABU   —Da droid is ready, Poe!
                    [*Babu turns C-3PO on. The droid's eyes*
                        glow red and he speaks in a low voice.
C-3PO   The Emperor's wayfinder is within
Th'Imperial vault, at delta three and six,
And transient nine three six, bearing three
Two on a moon in th'Endor system. Search   245
Ye from the southern shore. 'Tis only this
Blade tells. 'Tis only this blade tells.
                                [*C-3PO shuts down.*
BABU   —Hurrah!
FINN   The Endor system? Where the conflict last

Hath ended?

     [The workshop begins to rumble. Rey
     looks outside and sees a ship overhead.

REY   —Ren's Destroyer 'tis!

POE   —E'en here?

It haunts, of the wide world, this tiny spot?   250

REY   Another being sense I—and a friend!

'Tis Chewie!

FINN   —What of him? Grant us some hope!

REY   He is upon the ship, and there he lives!

POE   The world all love before thee if 'tis true,

Yet how?

REY   —Upon another transport he   255

Must have been hidden, taken, and flown hence!

POE   The resurrection of deep-buried faith

This news doth bring—we'll thither, rescue him!

ZORII   Thy friend doth ride upon that sky trash, Poe?

POE   A mystery of mysteries is he!   260

       [C-3PO awakens.

C-3PO   C-3PO am I, an expert in

The human-cyborg link. Who are you all?

POE   The void-like mem'ry of the golden one,

Whom I sincerely pity, may yet prove

A problem most severe.

BABU   —I Babu Frik!   265

C-3PO   Holla!

     [They all run outside, toward
     the Bestoon Legacy.

POE   —Move, Threepio, thy metal arse!

'Twere folly still to hope for higher heav'n,

Yet we are nearly to the ship return'd!

C-3PO   Speak thou so rudely, sir? We have just met!
ZORII   Poe, ere thou goest, take this token, please.   270
                          [She hands him the First Order
                                    captain's medallion.
             It may get thee aboard the cap'tal ship.
             Go ye, and help your friend.
POE   —Proud evening star!
             Methinks I cannot take this treasur'd gift.
ZORII   I care not what thou think'st.
REY   —Come, Poe, anon!
POE   [*to Zorii:*] This is the dawn of a most stormy life—   275
             Yet share it with us. Come withal, I pray.
ZORII   Get hence, kind Poe. Make haste.
POE   —Can I kiss thee,
             And drink the cup of pleasure to the dregs?
ZORII   Get hence, thou rogue! Show me how thou dost fly!
                          [Exeunt all but Zorii.
             So swiftly flew the man back to my life,   280
             So swiftly did the man depart again.
             Like lightning, briefly flashing in the night—
             Which, should one blink, the sight is wholly miss'd—
             With speed as this Poe Dameron is come,
             With speed as this Poe Dameron is gone.   285
             This cause in which he is entrench'd so deep
             Doth sway his heart more than my company,
             More than spice runners' coffers near at hand,
             More than the fellowship of our small gang.
             What is it, to believe in something so?   290
             Poe moves toward a nobler purpose found:
             A cause by justice, not by payment, built,
             A movement for which he would give his life.

Would that I may someday be mov'd as he,
To follow passion more than purse strings and   295
To do so with Poe Dam'ron by my side.
Another moment mayhap we shall find,
When turns the galaxy not unto war,
With ev'ry minute fraught with urgency
And danger knocking at each chamber door.   300
Then would I gladly look on him again,
And see what flowers blossom twixt we two.
Yet presently, I must away and hide,
Lest some far worser fate to me betide.

[Exit.

SCENE 1.

On Kylo Ren's command ship, the Steadfast.

Enter REY, POE DAMERON, FINN, C-3PO,
BB-8, *and* D-O *in the* Bestoon Legacy.

POE   The valuable medallion Zorii gave
             Hath work'd—we have been granted landing rights,
             And clear'd for entrance into hangar twelve.
             We shall into the ship, Chewbacca save,
             And fly before our band hath been observ'd.   5
             Then shall we join in the untainted mirth
             Of reunited friends.
REY   —O Chewie, be
             Thou patient, for we shall deliver thee.
C-3PO   Whoe'er this Chewie may be, madness 'tis!
                              [*The* Bestoon Legacy *flies inside
                                 a hangar of the* Steadfast.

Enter a few STORMTROOPERS *around the* Bestoon Legacy.

TROOPER 6   Credentials now present, and manifest.   10
                              [*Rey, Poe, and Finn emerge,
                                 shooting stormtroopers. The droids
                                 follow hesitantly behind.*
FINN   Feel ye our blaster fire, ye troubling knaves!
REY   [*to droids:*] You three, remain here with the ship.
C-3PO   —Forsooth!
             I fear my fellowship to die with ye.
POE   Forever changing places are these ships—

Finn, whither shall we go?

FINN   —Fain would I know,   15
But no idea have I. Yet follow on!

> *[They run aside while the droids*
> *wait with the ship.*

Enter TWO STORMTROOPERS, *pointing*
blasters at REY, POE, *and* FINN.

TROOPER 7   Drop ye your weapons, naughty ruffians!

> *[Rey uses a Jedi mind trick on them.*

REY   'Tis not a problem that we are herein.

TROOPER 7   'Tis not a problem that ye are herein.

TROOPER 8   Indeed, 'tis well!

REY   —You are reliev'd to see   20
Us on the ship.

TROOPER 7   —Hurrah that ye are here!

TROOPER 8   Most hearty welcome, gentles, to our ship.

POE   [*aside, to Finn:*] Is't possible, with a most knowing eye,
She plies such tricks on us?

REY   —We hither came
To find a prisoner and his things, too,   25
And ye shall help us in our noble search.

TROOPER 7   Proceed in the direction ye did run
And ye shall find th'interrogation room.

> *[Exeunt stormtroopers.*

FINN   They told us Chewie would be found this way—
Let us press forward, blasting cameras,   30
Until we locate Chewie finally.

> *[They come to a closed door and Finn*
> *begins working on the panel to open it.*

REY   [*aside:*] Again, the presence of another one
                   Doth call to me—the dagger is on board,
                   And I must thither if we would succeed.

                                   [Rey starts walking away as
                                   Finn opens the door.

FINN   Rey, swiftly come or we shall be undone.   35
REY   The dagger—it is here and we must have't.
POE   Perhaps it may be that my mind is wrought
                   To fever pitch, yet wherefore do we so?
REY   A feeling tells me, Poe. I prithee, meet
                   Me once more in the hangar.
FINN   —Foh, canst not—   40

                                   [Poe places a hand on Finn's chest,
                                   silencing him. Exit Rey.

POE   Be calm—I would not suffer, Finn, our thoughts
                   For any length of time to dwell upon
                   These latter speculations. Chewie is
                   Our goal and aim, so let us go anon.

They open another door. Enter CHEWBACCA *in his cell, bound.*

CHEWBAC.   Egh, auugh![20]
POE   —Of course we came! The novelty   45
                   Of an adventure such as this we would
                   Not miss, and never would leave thee behind.
CHEWBAC.   Egh, egh.[21]

---

[20] *Editor's translation:* My friends, ye came! I knew not if you would,
    For you have borrow'd peril great to do't.
    My Wookiee's heart doth praise your loyalty.
[21] *Editor's translation:* The dagger—we must find it presently!
    They stripp'd me of it when I came on board.

FINN   —Yea, Rey is with us, and shall find
                      The dagger ere we venture forth from here.

                      Enter ALLEGIANT GENERAL PRYDE *and various*
                      STORMTROOPERS *aside, in the hangar.*

PRYDE   Whose ship is this? Alert the legions stern—   50
                      Belike our enemies have hither come.
                                      [Exit Allegiant General Pryde as the
                                      stormtroopers begin searching the ship.
FINN   This way unto the ship, my friends. Make haste!
                              [The stormtroopers enter the corridor through
                                  which Poe, Finn, and Chewbacca are running.
TROOPER 9   'Tis them!

                                      [Finn shoots Trooper 9.
FINN   —Wrong way! Fie, they do swarm like bees!
POE   Nay, I could not have said this; it is an
                      Absurdity—there is no right way here!   55
                                      [The blaster fight continues as Poe,
                              Finn, and Chewbacca run toward the hangar,
                              encountering stormtroopers. Poe shoots one
                              stormtrooper and slides a blaster to Chewbacca.
                      Now, Chewie, thou mayst make thine own defense.
                      Are we yet near the hangar?
FINN   —'Tis not far.
                                      [Poe runs into an opening in the
                                      corridor and is shot in the arm.
                      Alack, good Poe! My truest confidant
                      Shot down in combat fierce. Say, art thou well?
                                      [Stormtroopers surround Poe,
                                          Finn, and Chewbacca.

POE   Although at times my pessimism dark   60
                 Hath been imputed to me as a crime,
                 I can say truly: nay, all is not well.
TROOPER 10   Freeze, scum, and drop your weapons on the ground!
POE   The ship and all within it are imbued
                 With spirit, gentles. You are well met!
TROOPER 10   —Tut!   65

            Enter GENERAL HUX *and* ALLEGIANT GENERAL PRYDE.

                 Allegiant General, th'Resistance rogues
                 We've apprehended, yet the scavenger
                 Is not with them.
PRYDE   —Pray, bear them from my sight
                 And terminate the scoundrels presently.
                                  [Exit Allegiant General Pryde.
                                  The stormtroopers take aim.
HUX   In troth, I'd gladly do the deed myself.   70
                 Give me thy blaster; I shall end their lives.
POE   *[aside, to Finn:]* I s'pose it is despair hath strung my
                                                                  nerves.
                 What was it thou had hop'd to say to Rey?
                                  [Trooper 10 hands Hux his blaster.
FINN   Are all thy feelings still consum'd with this?
POE   Is this an inconvenient time for thee?   75
                 Is't suddenly the case that thou dost fear
                 The consequences of discovery?
CHEWBAC.   Auugh!22

---

22 *Editor's translation:* The final moment of your little lives,
   And ye shall spend it dimly bickering?

FINN   —Not the best time, nay, for goodness' sake.
HUX   [*aside:*] The vast First Order searcheth for a spy.
              Who shall it be who will reveal the foe?   80
              If ye would ask, the answer comes: 'tis I.
              Intelligence from our strong ranks doth fly,
              And ev'rywhere around us tempers grow;
              The vast First Order searcheth for a spy.
              Who would be better thought of, by and by?   85
              Who would be proud his spirit true to show?
              If ye would ask, the answer comes: 'tis I.
              Strong Kylo Ren knows something is awry,
              With deep mistrust his visage is aglow—
              The vast First Order searcheth for a spy.   90
              Who can discern what future times are nigh?
              Who may envisage how events will go?
              If ye would ask, the answer comes: 'tis I.
              In future times, pray ask of Hux not why
              His heart hath turn'd, for it may cause him woe.   95
                        [*Hux shoots the stormtroopers.*
              [*To Finn, Poe, and Chewbacca:*] The vast First Order
                                        searcheth for a spy.
              If ye would ask, the answer comes: 'tis I.
POE   The shock that these few words, thus utterèd,
              Were so well calculated to convey!
FINN   E'en thee, our longtime foe?
HUX   —We've not much time.   100
POE   I'm not a little bit astonish'd to
              Discover it—I knew 'twas so, in faith!
FINN   In faith, thou never didst, ne'er could have guess'd.
                              [*Exeunt Poe Dameron, Finn,
                              Chewbacca, and General Hux.*

Enter REY *to* KYLO REN's *chamber.*

REY   A chamber full of light, and what is this?
                   Darth Vader's crush'd and broken mask—a-ha!   105
                   'Tis not a random room, 'tis Kylo Ren's!
                   Into his private chamber, I shall give
                   The full cause of my coming—take the knife
                   And Chewie's belt, and then depart at once.
                   Yet, even as my hand the dagger grasps,   110
                   The images of its foul deeds arise—
                   I hear the screams, the cries, the sadness that
                   This wicked instrument hath causèd. Nay.

        Enter KYLO REN *aside, on Kijimi but communicating*
                with REY *through the Force.*

KYLO	Rey—wheresoe'er thou be, art hard to find.
REY	And thou most difficult to be rid of, 115
	As though a parasite and I thy host.
KYLO	I push'd thee in the desert for one cause:
	I needed to see thee, and needed thee
	To see the untold truth of who thou art.
	I know thy story, ev'ry detail worth. 120
	Rey—
REY	—Thou dost lie.
KYLO	—Ne'er have I lied to thee.
	Thy parents were nobody by design—
	Such was their choice, which they did make to keep
	Thee safe.
REY	—Do not presume to speak of them!
KYLO	Thou dost remember more than thou admitt'st. 125
	I was inside thy head.
REY	—I want not this!
KYLO	Explore thy memories and thou shalt—
REY	—Nay!

*[Rey attacks him with her
lightsaber and they duel.*

KYLO	Remember them!
REY	[*aside:*] —Unbidden, lo, they come!
	The face of my dear mother, sore afeard,
	Embracing me, insisting I be brave. 130
	My father, too, assuring me that I
	Would safer be, remaining on Jakku.
	His promise ere they left in Ochi's ship,
	My mournful cries as they departed thence.
KYLO	They sold thee to protect thee.
REY	—Stop thy mouth! 135

KYLO   I know what did befall them afterward.
                                        [They continue dueling.
           Tell me where thou art hiding. Thou know'st not
           The story in its ev'ry twist and turn—
           'Twas Palpatine who had thy parents ta'en.
           He search'd for thee, yet they would not reveal   140
           Thy whereabouts. Thus order'd he their deaths.

REY   [*aside:*] In my mind's eye I see the tragic scene:
           My mother telling Ochi that I was
           Not on Jakku, and moments later he—
           Pernicious criminal—my father slew!   145
                  *[Rey and Kylo Ren duel more, and in the
                    process they knock over the pedestal where
                        Vader's mask rests. Kylo Ren sees it.*

KYLO   A-ha! My chamber, then, is where thou art.
                                                [They duel.
           Thou knowest why the Emperor hath e'er
           Desir'd thy death.

REY   —Nay.

KYLO   —I shall thither fly
           And tell thee in the flesh. 'Twill better be.
                  [Exit Kylo Ren. Rey runs toward the hangar.

           Enter STORMTROOPERS, *approaching the droids in the hangar.*

TROOPER 11 Who are ye and what is your purpose here?   150
           [*To C-3PO:*] What is thine operating number, droid?

C-3PO   Nokito wahnga wan.

TROOPER 11   —'Tis language none!
                  [Rey runs in, shooting the stormtroopers.

C-3PO   O! My first laser battle. What a life!

REY   Where are the others?
C-3PO   —They have not return'd.

Enter KYLO REN, *flying into the hangar in his TIE whisper.*

REY   I prithee, find them! Get thee gone at once!   155
                          [The droids run down the halls of the ship.
D-O   Ahead, our friends!
C-3PO   —Indeed, I see them come!

Enter POE DAMERON, FINN, CHEWBACCA, *and*
GENERAL HUX, *heading for a second hangar.*

HUX   Th'impeders I've shut down, yet not for long—
             Ye have mere seconds to escape the ship.
POE   I do not hesitate to say that I'm
             Amaz'd, can scarcely credit mine own sense—   160
             The *Falcon*! She is here, survivor strong!
                          [Exeunt Poe Dameron, Chewbacca, C-3PO,
                          BB-8, and D-O into the second hangar,
                          where the Millennium Falcon *awaits.*
HUX   [*to Finn:*] Wait, prithee. Blast me quickly in the arm.
FINN   Yet wherefore should I injure thee e'en thus?
HUX   An thou dost not, they'll know 'twas I who help'd.
                          [Finn shoots Hux in the leg.
FINN   Why art thou proffering thine aid to us?   165
HUX   It matters not to me if ye do win—
             I only hope that Kylo Ren will lose.
                          [Exit Finn to the hangar. Exit General
                          Hux separately. In the other hangar,
                          Rey approaches Kylo Ren.

Enter STORMTROOPERS, *watching the standoff.*

REY   The scene is set, the stage arrang'd for thee.
             I charge thee, by thy reverence for truth,
             Here to unfold—although thou didst intend   170
             To keep in darkness what occasion now
             Reveals before 'tis ripe—what thou dost know.
             Say wherefore th'Emperor did hunt for me.
             Why would he track and kill a child? Pray, tell!

KYLO   Foresaw he what thou wouldst, in time, become.   175
             Thou hast not merely pow'r—thou hast his pow'r.
             Thou art his granddaughter, a Palpatine.
             My mother was to Vader daughter born,
             Thy father was the Emperor's own son.

                              [Kylo Ren begins walking toward
                                Rey, who backs away from him,
                                approaching the edge of the hangar.

             What Palpatine doth not yet understand   180
             Is that we are a dyad in the Force—
             We two are one. Together, we shall kill
             Dread Palpatine and take the throne at last.
             Thou know'st what thou must do, thou knowest well.

                              [Kylo Ren takes off his mask and
                                extends his hand to Rey.

REY   Forsooth. I shall do ev'rything I ought.   185

Enter POE DAMERON, FINN, CHEWBACCA, C-3PO, BB-8,
and D-O *in the* Millennium Falcon, *flying next to the*
hangar. STORMTROOPERS *begin firing on the* Falcon.

POE   With a rapidity that will surprise,

I'll blow the lot asunder—steady, hold!
> *[Poe pulls a lever, engaging the thrusters*
> *and pushing the stormtroopers back.*
> *Kylo Ren holds his ground. Finn stands*
> *on the* Falcon's *boarding ramp.*

FINN   Rey, fly anon! Abscond while yet thou canst!
> *[Rey jumps to Finn, who grabs her*
> *and helps her inside the* Millennium
> Falcon. *Exeunt Rey, Poe Dameron, Finn,*
> *Chewbacca, C-3PO, BB-8, and D-O.*

KYLO   Though thou this confrontation wouldst delay,
           The cat will mew, and dog will have his day.   190
> *[Exeunt Kylo Ren and stormtroopers.*

SCENE 2.

On Kylo Ren's command ship, the Steadfast.

Enter GENERAL HUX, ALLEGIANT GENERAL PRYDE,
and various OFFICERS *and* STORMTROOPERS.

HUX   Coordinated the incursion was,
           Allegiant General. They did o'erpow'r
           The guards and forcèd me to escort them
           Directly to the ship.

PRYDE   —All now is clear.
           [*To Trooper 12:*] Hail thou our Supreme Leader
                                          presently.   5

TROOPER 12 Yea, sir.
> *[Pryde takes Trooper 12's blaster and*
> *shoots Hux. General Hux dies.*

PRYDE —Inform him that the spy is found.
On vengeance shall misprision run aground.

[Exeunt.

SCENE 3.

On the Millennium Falcon *and on Kef Bir.*

Enter REY.

REY If revelations were a currency,
A wealthy woman should I be indeed.
Misfortune, though, is mine inheritance.
The Emperor's granddaughter, is it so?
Here is prosperity I wanted not.   5
Entangl'd now his story is with mine,
Knit are our threads of fate with strands of blood.
I did prefer my former poverty,
Not knowing that my parents had the wealth
Of parentage and ancestry to boast.   10
Fie! This unask'd-for affluence doth reek.
Perturbing birthright, legacy of filth,
As if the drops of Palpatine's rank blood
Let loose within my veins were naught but bile,
Polluting any good with utter hate.   15
And Kylo Ren, what shall I do with him?
The words he spoke—that we a dyad are—
Is't possible he may be credited?
Ne'er did I hope to join our two accounts,
E'en when his offer is the galaxy.   20
Rey is not Ren, yet what shall Rey then be?

Eventually, riches come to naught—
Vain is the hope that rests on pedigree.
I must not take the path of th'Emperor—
Let me not on such borrow'd wealth rely.   25
Endow'd with Jedi wisdom, peace, and strength,
Depend on this: I'll pay to each their due.

Enter POE DAMERON *and* CHEWBACCA *aside, in the cockpit.*

POE   They follow not, which turneth my heart cold:
               Insufferable gloom pervades my spir't.
CHEWBAC.   Egh, egh.[23]
POE   —The landing gear is broken? What?   30
               What nonsense dost thou talk! To what degree?
               [*Calling:*] Finn, Rey, can ye assist? It seemeth our
               Ability to land is dubious.

Enter FINN.

FINN   Let us attempt to fix the landing gear,
               That we not fail for want of softer ground.   35
REY   Obtaining the wayfinder is our sole
               Objective; finding Exegol is all.
FINN   'Tis what we do pursue e'en now, in faith.
REY   He kill'd my mother and my father, too—
               I shall find Palpatine and him destroy.   40
FINN   These words have not the sound of thee, sweet Rey.
               Full well I know thee—

---

[23] *Editor's translation:* Belike they deem us doom'd to failure, since
    The landing gear severely broken is.

REY   —Thus do many say.
          How many people lately say they know
          Precisely who Rey is? I am afeard
          None know who Rey is truly, in her soul.   45
                    [Rey and Finn brace themselves as the
                    Millennium Falcon *crash-lands on Kef Bir.*

Enter EMPEROR PALPATINE, *in beam, and* KYLO REN *on balcony.*

PALPATINE   Th'apprentice of the Jedi liveth yet.
          Perchance thou hast betray'd me. Is it so?
          Make me not turn my fleet upon thine own.
KYLO   I know where she is bound, and shall pursue.
          She ne'er shall be a Jedi.
PALPATINE   —Make it so!   50
          Be certain of thy words. Kill her at once.
                    [*Exeunt Emperor Palpatine and Kylo Ren.*

Enter C-3PO, BB-8, *and* D-O *as they disembark
from the* Millennium Falcon *with* REY, POE, FINN,
and CHEWBACCA. *They walk to the shore and behold
remnants of the second Death Star in the water.*

D-O   Say! What is that?
REY   —The Death Star, what remains.
          An evil place, left o'er from war of old.
POE   If ever island were enchanted, this
          Is it. An island made of steel and brick—   55
          Look on the size of it. We shall be years
          In searching for the thing we need within.
C-3PO   Dear, dear!

REY   —"'Tis only this blade tells." Those words
Shall prove a clue unto our purpose true.
        [Rey pulls Ochi's dagger from her satchel.
Perhaps a point along the hilt—a-ha!   60
        [She pulls a small extension
            from the dagger's hilt.
The blade shall tell us ev'rything, methinks.
        [She scans the Death Star with the blade
        until she finds a point where the shape of the
        blade matches the shape of the wreckage.
We'll find our way to the wayfinder there.

Enter JANNAH *and her band of* WARRIORS, *riding* ORBAKS.

POE   This island is a very sing'lar one—
The Death Star first, now threats at ev'ry side.
Beware, my friends, here comes a troubling band.   65

                              [Poe and Finn point their blasters
                                        at Jannah and her crew.

JANNAH   Harsh landing, worthies.

POE   —Would a madman have
Been e'en so wise as this, to land it thus?
Still, worse I've seen.

JANNAH   —And better have I seen.
Are ye from the Resistance hither come?

POE   Mine answer doth depend upon yourselves.   70
Are ye but demons that exult in the
Damnation of your foes? Who are ye? Tell!

JANNAH   Transmission we receiv'd from someone known
As Babu Frik.

C-3PO   —One of mine oldest friends!

JANNAH   He said ye would come hither, and that you   75
Our final hope do represent. Is't so?

REY   We must unto the wreckage of the base.
There's aught within that we must needs obtain.

JANNAH   By water I can take ye thitherward.

FINN   Hast seen the water? For 'tis rough and wild.   80

JANNAH   Yea, presently 'tis much too dangerous.
E'en when the morning sun shall raise his car
Above the border of th'horizon, then
We may make our approach.

REY   —We cannot wait.
We've no time.

POE   —Nor, it seems, a choice. In the   85
Consideration of the faculties
And impulses that overcome our toss'd
And wearied minds, let us this respite take.
Let us unto the ship and make repairs.

    [*To Jannah:*] Have ye spare parts?

JANNAH   —Some, aye. I'm

              Jannah call'd. 90

    [*All proceed to the* Millennium Falcon *to*
      work on the ship except Rey, who exits.

C-3PO   [*to Poe:*] A dreadful situation in th'extreme.

    Is ev'ry day with thy lot similar?

    'Tis madness.

POE   [*to Chewbacca:*]   —Pray, remind me, Chewie: did

    We find a way his volume to control?

    What doth he mean by yowling in that kind   95

    Of style, e'en like a catty-mount?

CHEWBAC.   —Egh, auugh!²⁴

    [*Elsewhere in the ship, Jannah*
      hands a part to Finn.

JANNAH Take thou this part—an oh-six, yet should suit.

FINN   Full thanks. Yet, hold—for something seems amiss.

    The provenance of this, thy proffer'd part,

    Is't not from the First Order?

JANNAH   —Even so.   100

    There is a cruiser old on our west ridge,

    Which we have stripp'd of parts. 'Twas once our own—

    The one to which my band was once assign'd,

    The one in which my band did once abscond.

FINN   Amazement plentiful o'ercomes my heart—   105

    Were ye of th'rank First Order?

JANNAH   —Not by choice.

    Conscripted as mere children were we all;

---

²⁴ *Editor's translation:* Would that we might, for I have had enow
  Of prattling from the empty-headed droid!

	Tee-zed-one-sev'n-one-nine was once my name,	
	If e'er a number could be call'd a name.	
FINN	Eff-en-two-one-eight-seven was mine own!	110
JANNAH	E'en thou?	
FINN	—Ne'er knew I any but myself	
	Who from the vile First Order did abscond.	
JANNAH	Deserters, yea! Each one of us was once	
	A stormtrooper. 'Twas at the battle fought	
	On Ansett Island—there we mutinied	115
	Together, after we were told to fire	
	Upon civilians, which our consciences	
	Could ne'er allow. We could not do the deed,	
	And laid our weapons down with single mind.	
FINN	Indeed? The lot of ye?	
JANNAH	—The company	120
	Entire. In retrospect, impossible	
	It is to say how the collective act	
	Took root in ev'ry heart and mind as one.	
	'Twas no decision—	
FINN	—Born of instinct pure.	
	A feeling.	
JANNAH	—Yea, a feeling.	
FINN	—'Twas the Force.	125
	The Force did lead me here, among this group,	
	To Rey and Poe, my dearest friends in th'world.	
JANNAH	Thou speak'st as if thou knewest it were real.	
FINN	'Tis real. I need no evidence thereof—	
	At first I was not certain, yet am now.	130
	None but the Force could lead me unto them,	
	None but the Force could power so much hope,	
	None but the Force could guide our searching steps,	

None but the Force, which binds, surrounds, protects.
[They walk aside. BB-8 approaches Poe.

BB-8   [*to Poe:*] Blox flewflig rooh zood bleerooq flir zilf blee 135
Reej flliflit blis blav flirzooz bleeflib blay?

POE   What dost thou mean, to ask of where Rey is?
Hast thou not seen her? Raise alarum bells,
Their tintinnabulation shall resound—
A world of solemn thought their melody   140
Compels—Finn, Jannah, come! Rey's fled and gone!
[All rush outside. Finn uses
quadnoculars to spot Rey.

FINN   My lass of folly rides upon the sea!
Such waves she faceth, nearly tipping o'er.
So unforgiving is this tempest grave,
I fear our Rey shall soon a shadow be.   145

JANNAH   Took she a skimmer? Brave and foolish both.

POE   By hell, what was she thinking of? She who
So well doth know the nature of my soul
Could not suppose her act would make me glad.

FINN   'Tis plain: we must go after her anon.   150

POE   Her actions make my nerves and spirit sick—
Sick unto death with that long agony.
We shall repair the *Falcon* and go forth
To rescue her when first we're able to.

FINN   Nay, if we wait so long, she shall be lost.   155

POE   'Twas she who left her friends behind, afeard—
A pile of nothing but commingl'd gloom.
What wouldst thou do, Finn, swim?

FINN   —She's not herself.
Thou knowest not the demons she doth face,
The battles she is fighting deep within.   160

POE   Yet thou dost, eh? So happy, dauntless, and
           Sagacious art thou, that thou know'st e'en this?
FINN   In faith, I do, as Leia also doth.
POE   The truth should be inviolate above
           All things, e'en this: I am not Leia, Finn.   165
FINN   With damnèd certainty thou speak'st not false.
JANNAH   [aside, to Finn:] Come thou with me. Another skimmer I
           Can offer thee, an thou wouldst take the risk.

                                          [Exeunt all but Poe.

POE   Ah, dream too bright to last! His words, they sting;
           O, Finn, the friend—nay brother—of my heart,   170
           I would that we were not at odds herein.
           Friends have I known throughout my blessèd span,
           Close allies, confidants most plentiful,
           Yet none were so well suited to myself
           As thou wert from the moment we first met.   175
           Thou art the other half who makes me whole,
           As one doth think of Poe, one thinks of Finn.
           Thou art the voice that doth my sentence end,
           Before I speak it, thou dost fill it in.
           Thou art the map that puts me back on course,   180
           When I veer wide, thou settest me aright.
           Thou art the books, the arts, the academes,
           That show, contain, and nourish all the world.
           Apologies, dear Finn, I owe to thee,
           For my hotheaded and quick-temper'd bile—   185
           I am the fire, thou art refreshing rain,
           And once again I need thine easing cool.
           Let us, when we are mad, not stay so long,
           That sooner and that sweeter comes the time
           When our two minds united are again,   190

The glad reunion of two wills in one.
This storm that passes by us shall surcease,
The sunshine break upon a greater peace.

                                                      [*Exit.*

SCENE 4.

On the second Death Star.

Enter REY, *who begins to climb.*

REY   Years on their years have pass'd since this bleak base
             Exploded into pieces o'er the air.
             The shell of it is harsh and horrible;
             In shades of gray and gloom its ghosts reside.
             Ne'er did I, as a child upon Jakku,   5
             Think ever I would see the very place—
             Here where the Empire ended years ago.
             Exciting 'twere, if not so dangerous,
             Fantastic that I should such hist'ry touch,
             Observing it with ev'ry sense I have.   10
             Rehearse thou not thy wonder longer, Rey—
             Climb, rather, t'ward the end thou must achieve.
             Experience doth make a simpler task—
             Perforce I have turn'd scavenger once more.
             Recall the steps, maneuvers, placement that   15
             Once I relied upon for daily bread.
             Fear not, but cautious be, for in this wreck
             One small mistake may quickly fatal prove.
             Unto the level accurate I've come,
             Now through this hall, with vacant helmets strewn.   20

Dread filleth me—here is the Emp'ror's throne,
Pulsating with the Force like mine own blood.
How now? A door doth open, bidding me—
     [A door opens. Rey walks through
       and it closes behind her.
Enclosing me e'en as I step within.
Night is not dark as 'tis within this room,   25
Obscuring outer sight and inner calm.
Methinks I nearer draw unto—a-ha!
E'en there, the wayfinder before me lies.
No trap awaits above or underneath—
Oblique the path that led me to the goal,   30
Naught here but rubble, darkness, shades, and fear.

 She grasps the wayfinder. Enter DARK REY,
 brandishing a double-bladed lightsaber.

DARK REY Rey, never be afeard of who thou art.
            [They duel.

REY   O, ghoulish vision born of hell's own heart!
     I yet may change these shadows I have seen.
       [Dark Rey snarls at Rey. Frightened, Rey
        stumbles backward into the former throne
        room. Exit Dark Rey. Rey drops the wayfinder.

 Enter KYLO REN, *picking up the wayfinder.*

KYLO   Look thou upon thyself, and be asham'd.   35
     Thou wouldst prove to my mother that thou art
     A Jedi, heir to that proud legacy.
     Instead, herein thou provest something else.

> Thou canst make no return unto her now—
> E'en as thou didst depart Jakku to make   40
> A new life with the weak Resistance, thou
> Hast made departure secondary here,
> And never shall go back into their fold.
> See, thou and I are one—I also have
> Ta'en steps that led me permanently from   45
> The life that once I led, in former times.

REY   Give me the wayfinder.

KYLO   —The dark side doth
> Reside within our very natures, Rey.
> Submit thereto.

REY   —Give me the wayfinder.

KYLO   Thou never shalt proceed to Exegol   50
> Unless thou ventur'st forth withal myself.
>   *[He crushes the wayfinder in his hand.*

REY   Nay, villain!
>   *[She brandishes her lightsaber. They duel.*

KYLO   *[aside:]*   —Dodge and sidestep, yet she doth
> Stiffen the sinews, summon up the blood,
> Disguise fair nature with hard-favor'd rage,
> Then lend the eye a terrible aspect.   55
>   *[Kylo Ren turns on his lightsaber and
>   jumps outside, onto the wreckage
>   by the sea. Rey pursues him.*

> *Enter* GENERAL LEIA ORGANA *on balcony.*
> *Enter* R2-D2 *and* MAZ KANATA *on balcony, aside.*

LEIA   What shadows spread their darkness o'er my sight!
> The Force speaks in clear visions unto me:

My son and mine adopted daughter caught
In conflict vicious, battling to the death.
MAZ   [*to R2-D2:*] Behold, she plumbs the boundless depths of
                 grief!   60

I'd have not such a heart within my breast
E'en for the dignity of the whole body.
'Tis certain Leia knows what she must do,
Artoo—to reach her errant son she must
Expend whatever strength in her remains.   65
R2-D2   Beep, hoo. [*Aside:*] My lady and my general!
                [*Rey and Kylo Ren continue to*
                duel on a section of the Death Star
                surrounded by water on both sides.

Enter FINN *and* JANNAH, *aside.*

FINN   Fraught was the skimmer journey by the sea,
Yet we—though tempest-toss'd—forfended death.
Now may I proffer help unto her. [*Calling:*] Rey!
REY   [*aside:*] I'll not have Finn in danger, standing twixt   70
This villain and myself. Nay, Finn, away!
                [*Rey uses the Force to shove Finn away,*
                then continues to duel Kylo Ren.
KYLO   [*aside:*] A massive wave shall break upon our heads,
As if all nature thunder'd at our clash
And would the conflict settle equally,
By washing us beneath the ocean deep.   75
                [*Rey jumps from one part of the*
                wreckage to another much farther away.
                Kylo follows her. They land in a place
                Jannah and Finn cannot reach.

JANNAH   [*aside:*] They leap like gods, not humans, by my troth.
FINN   [*aside:*] Though I perceive the Force, 'tis not yet thus:
            Here is a power far beyond my ken.
                              [*Rey and Kylo continue to duel.*
REY   Thou villain! One of us shall not depart—
            'Tis only Rey or Kylo shall go forth.   80
                              [*Finn tries to run toward Rey.*
JANNAH   Thou canst not follow them—most certainly
            The sea would sweep thee up like thou wert chaff.
FINN   Unhand me, I shall not forsake her!
JANNAH   —Nay!
            Hear reason, or thou shalt be quite destroy'd.
FINN   O Rey, would that I could thy safety win!   85
REY   [*aside:*] Our skill and pow'r is match'd most perfectly.
KYLO   [*aside:*] Our acumen and strength are nearly twins.
                              [*She takes a giant leap to another
                              part of the wreckage, closer to where
                              Kylo Ren's TIE whisper sits.*
REY   [*aside:*] I dive again, but he will follow on.
KYLO   [*aside:*] She dives again; I shall with purpose stride.
                              [*He walks and catches up to her.*
REY   [*aside:*] The final confrontation, blow for blow!   90
KYLO   [*aside:*] The final confrontation, come what may.
REY   [*aside:*] He tries to strike, I stop him by the Force.
KYLO   [*aside:*] She tries to swipe, the dark side stoppeth her.
REY   [*aside:*] A dyad certainly, if e'er there was.
KYLO   [*aside:*] The realization of our fates conjoin'd   95
            Doth break upon her face, e'en as these waves
            Come crashing o'er the ramparts hereabout.
            She knoweth she shall ne'er defeat me here,
            For we are unified at ev'ry point.

[*As they duel, Rey collapses to her
knees in exhaustion. Kylo raises
his lightsaber to strike her.*

LEIA [*calling softly:*] O Ben, my boy, my son, a mother's bliss. 100
[*Leia lies down. Kylo Ren pauses, looking
backward, and drops his lightsaber.*

REY [*aside:*] The error I have long awaited. Strike!
[*Rey ignites Kylo Ren's lightsaber
and runs him through with it.*

LEIA Exchange forgiveness with me, noble Ben:
Mine and thy father's death come not on thee.
[*Leia dies.*

REY [*aside:*] Nay, nay! The voice that call'd him reacheth
me—
My teacher, guide, and friend, my General! 105
O Leia, can it be that thou art gone?
[*Rey turns off Kylo Ren's lightsaber, and he falls.*

R2-D2 [*aside, singing:*] Come away, come away, death,
And in sad cypress let her be laid.
Fly away, fly away, breath;
She is slain by grief that doth not fade. 110
Her shroud of white, stuck all with yew,
O, prepare it!
Her part of death, no one so true
Did share it.

REY [*aside:*] What have I done? This gentle lad laid low, 115
Who is the only vestige, now, of her.
Shall I give my life for an enemy's?
Shall sacrifice become mine epitaph?
But is he, rightly said, mine enemy?
And would I ask a fonder epitaph? 120

If I may healing proffer, yea—I shall,
In mourning for my Leia, gone too soon,
I'll render back the son that once she lost.

        [Rey places her hand on Kylo Ren's
         injury and transfers life to him
         through the Force. He is healed.

KYLO   *[aside:]* This touch—an unexpected clemency!
     My wound is gone. Thus hath she done for me.   125

REY   'Twas true that once I long'd to take thy hand,
     Yet not the hand of Kylo Ren. Ben's hand,
     Such would I gladly take if tender'd me.

        [She runs to Kylo Ren's TIE whisper
         and flies away. Exit Rey.

FINN   She flies, and I no succor furnish'd her,
     She flies, and even thus I'm left behind,   130
     She flies, confusion reigning in her heart,
     She flies, and I know not where she hath gone.
     Dark moment for my true companion Rey,
     Who seeketh separation from her friends
     And flees with troubl'd heart and weary mind.   135

        [The Millennium Falcon *appears to*
         bear Finn and Jannah away.

     May fate ordain that we shall meet again.
     Conferr'd I not what thou didst need today,
     Yet Finn declares: I'll make it up some way.

        [Exeunt Finn and Jannah in the
        Millennium Falcon. *On the balcony,*
        R2-D2 and Maz approach Leia's body.

MAZ   Thou antic death, which laugh'st us here to scorn,
     Anon from thine insulting tyranny,   140
     Coupled in bonds of perpetuity,

One Leia, wingèd through the lither sky,
In thy despite shall scape mortality.
Goodnight, sweet princess, angel of our hearts.

> [*Exeunt Maz Kanata and R2-D2. Leia's*
> *body remains on the balcony.*

KYLO   Alone, directionless yet still alive,   145
        I am abandon'd on this sopping steel.

Enter GHOST OF HAN SOLO.

HAN   Holla, my child. O, how I miss thee, boy.
KYLO   Thy son is dead.
HAN   —Nay, Kylo Ren is dead.
        My son, my boy, my Ben—he liveth yet.
KYLO   Thou art a memory, and nothing more.   150
        Thou art, mayhap, some undigested beef,
        Thou art more gravy than come from the grave.
HAN   Yea, 'tis thy memory whence I have come.

Come home.

KYLO   —Nay, 'tis too late, for she is gone.

HAN   Thy mother, truly, she is gone indeed.   155
Yet all that she did stand for whilst she liv'd,
And ev'rything for which she bravely fought,
'Tis not gone, and with thee it ne'er shall be.
Ben, hear me, please.

KYLO   —I know what I must do,
Yet fear I've not the strength to make it so.   160

HAN   Thou dost and e'er didst.

KYLO   —Father! I—

HAN   —I know.

[Kylo Ren turns around and throws his
lightsaber into the sea. Exit Ghost of Han Solo.

KYLO   Now I have taken heart thou vanishest:
Sweet spirit, I would hold more talk with thee.
This visitation marks a turning point:
The end of one life as another starts.   165
I must be strong, remember my first call,
And shun the folly that consum'd my life.
The years spent with the vile First Order shall
Become the nadir of a human life,
The lowest rung upon my ladder tall,   170
The ebbing of the ocean of my days,
The bass notes of the symphony of time.
However long my strand of life shall be
Ere fate ordains to clip it and release
My life into the Force forevermore,   175
I shall exist to bring light to the world,
Deliver hope to those too long oppress'd,
Make recompense for all the wrong I've done.

The work beginneth now, as I proceed
To Exegol to face the Emperor.   180
Defeating him must be th'initial deed
In making up for Kylo Ren's foul works.
The name doth leave a rotten taste inside
My mouth—what vanity, to turn away
The name my loving parents proffer'd me.   185
No evil knave, no longer Kylo Ren,
I turn away from he who I was then—
From now, I am a Solo once again,
The son of Han and Leia—I am Ben!

                                                       [Exit.

ACT IV

SCENE 1.

Aboard the Steadfast.

Enter two STORMTROOPERS.

TROOPER 7	Good morrow, mate. Thy face is bonny as
	The morning sun when first it shineth bright.
TROOPER 8	Well met to thee as well. I see thou art
	In spirits high with smile upon thy face—
	Or so, beneath thy helmet, I presume. 5
TROOPER 7	I cannot keep my merriment from thee!
TROOPER 8	What is it that hath fill'd thee so with joy?
TROOPER 7	I have been in the bunkroom. Ah—I find
	Myself embarrass'd suddenly to tell
	Of what I did therein.
TROOPER 8	—Embarrass'd? Thou? 10
	'Tis only I, thy best and oldest friend.
TROOPER 7	We two were station'd here together but
	A fortnight past, and only then did meet.
TROOPER 8	And yet our shar'd experience, when we
	Were swindl'd by that Jedi harpy—
TROOPER 7	—True! 15
	No truer friend I've had since that occurr'd.
TROOPER 8	Wilt thou vouchsafe thy secret, then, to me?
TROOPER 7	If thou shalt promise ne'er to mock, sirrah.
TROOPER 8	Say never so, my friend. I mock thee? Ha!
	What was it, in the bunkroom, thou wert at? 20
	'Twas naught nefarious or aberrant?
TROOPER 7	Nay, nay—'twas but a pastime, which is yet
	A newfound hobby, vulnerable still.
TROOPER 8	I see, friend. Fear thou not my confidence—

Mine ears shall hear and ne'er a mock be born   25
From those two organs, to escape my mouth.
TROOPER 7 The plain fact is, I took some time to write.
TROOPER 8 To write? Heard I aright?
TROOPER 7   —A holy rite,
Composing with my pen, mine ink, and wit.
TROOPER 8 I am astonishèd! What dost thou write?   30
Belike some tome—the epic history
Of our First Order, in its chapter first?
TROOPER 7 Nay, something else, which still my tongue would hide.
TROOPER 8 Proceed, I pray—pull thou the bandage off.
TROOPER 7 'Tis fiction that I write! Yea! Stories, tales,   35
A fancy of imagination pure.
TROOPER 8 E'en so? Is't something I could ever read?
TROOPER 7 Nay, never, no. 'Tis wholly private. Nay.
TROOPER 8 Canst thou, at least, tell me what thou didst write
That put thee in this splendid, joyful mood?   40
TROOPER 7 This far I'll tell thee, yea, though nothing more:
I am the author of an epic tale,
Writ in nine parts, an opera of space
That telleth such adventures and delights
Thou never wouldst believe I penn'd the thing.   45
TROOPER 8 The tale sounds marvelous. How shall it end?
TROOPER 7 I cannot tell.
TROOPER 8   —Thou canst tell me, in sooth.
TROOPER 7 Thou miss'st my meaning utterly, my friend—
I merely mean I do not know as yet.
These strands, unravel'd, spread most anywhere—   50
Respect I've learn'd for storytellers all
Who plot these tales and tie up ev'ry end.
TROOPER 8 Full confidence have I thou shalt do so

As well. It seemeth art is thy domain,
Not mine, and I do wish thee well of it.   55
One day, perchance thou shalt let me peruse
The chronicle—once thou completest it.
Until that time, shall we to supper go?

TROOPER 7   Yea. Writing e'er gives me an appetite!

                                      [Exeunt.

        Enter EMPEROR PALPATINE, *in beam, and*
           ALLEGIANT GENERAL PRYDE.

PALPATINE   The princess of old Alderaan did thwart   60
              My plan, and still her deeds shall be in vain.

Come unto Exegol, strong Gen'ral Pryde.

PRYDE   As I did serve you in the former wars,
I serve you now, to settle former scores.

PALPATINE   Take thou the ship unto a world they know   65
And let it burn, our dominance to show.
The Final Order doth begin anon.
She'll come to us; her friends shall follow on.

PRYDE   With full allegiance I give you my yea,
And shall your bidding do sans more delay.   70

[Exeunt.

Enter CHORUS.

CHORUS   Behold, the power once in Death Star hands
Is wielded by a single ship alone.
A Star Destroyer's weaponry expands
And zounds! Kijimi unto bits is blown.

[Exit.

SCENE 2.
On Ajan Kloss.

Enter POE DAMERON, FINN, CHEWBACCA, C-3PO,
BB-8, *and* D-O *emerging from the* Millennium Falcon.
Enter COMMANDER D'ACY, *meeting them.*

D'ACY   Poe, Finn, ye have return'd—with heavy heart
I must unfold to ye what hath occur'd—

FINN   We have some haste, Commander; hold thou off.

POE   We must unto the general anon.

                    Our news for her is most indefinite   5
                    And altogether unaccountable.
D'ACY   Yet she is gone and cannot hear your suit.
CHEWBAC.   Auugh, auugh![25]
FINN   —Nay, Chewie, be not lost in grief!
CHEWBAC.   Auugh, auugh, auugh, auugh![26]

        Enter ROSE TICO, LIEUTENANT CONNIX, *and* BEAUMONT KIN.

D'ACY   —The woes but multiply.
                    We have receiv'd intelligence of late: 10

---

[25] *Editor's translation:* My princess and my general, not so!
[26] *Editor's translation:* There is no cease of sorrow when the heart
    Like refuse is cast out and thrown away.
    My best friend, Han, was fell'd by his own son,
    And now is reunited with his love—
    The woman who such kindness show'd to me,
    She who was ever noble, graceful, true,
    More than a friend: my human family.
    When she walk'd into our two scoundrel lives—
    Brash, certain of herself, and calling me
    A walking carpet moments after we
    Our first encounter had on Death Star old—
    I was not certain we could ever be
    E'en allies, far less comrades closely knit.
    The years and our shar'd cause smooth'd ev'ry edge
    Of our beginning, rocky though it was.
    In time, her wit and grit fit perfectly,
    The piece that did complete our puzzle well.
    Then were we Leia, Han, Chewbacca, Luke,
    Profound quartet t'amaze a galaxy.
    Han fallen, Luke did follow, Leia now—
    On sorrow have I surfeited too much,
    Ate too much of the bitter meat of woe.
    Shall old Chewbacca outlive ev'ryone?
    Hath no man's dagger here a point for me?

The vile First Order sack'd Kijimi whole—
The planet blasted into shards of stone.

POE   Kijimi? How? First Leia and now this?
[*Aside:*] This will be sure to cut me to the heart—
The place where my true Bliss resideth. O!   15

D'ACY   A blast from one mere Star Destroyer, Poe,
One of the newfound ships of the Sith fleet
Come forward from the unknown regions grim.

BEAUMONT   The Emp'rer sent a ship from Exegol.
Doth this, perforce, mean each ship in the fleet—   20

POE   Hath planet-killing weapons, yea, 'tis plain.
Upon this subject, however, shall I
Forbear to dilate. This is how he shall
The war forever end.

ROSE   —Take heed, I pray:
The strange transmission doth appear upon   25
Each frequency the radio can call.

        [*A strange voice comes out of Rose's radio.*

BEAUMONT   [*translating:*] The vile Resistance now is dead. The fire
That burneth by the power of the Sith
Shall blaze. All worlds surrender or be slain.
The Final Order doth begin today.   30

ROSE   [*to Poe:*] Our Leia made thee acting general.
I prithee, guide us. Say, what shall we do?

POE   Let me collect my thoughts awhile, good Rose.
Exhausted, very nat'rally, by such
Stupendous efforts, would I spend some time   35
In contemplation of our circumstance.

        [*Poe walks aside. Finn approaches D-O, who
          is rummaging through Rey's belongings.*

FINN   Nay, fain would I not have thee touch these things,

For they belong unto my treasur'd friend.

D-O   O, sorry! She is gone?

FINN   —Yea, fled and gone.
       I know not where she's flown.

D-O   —I miss her, yea!   40

FINN   Thy feeling's mine—I miss her sorely, too.
       What is thy name, thou frisky little droid?

                    [Finn and D-O continue to speak. Poe,
                    aside, looks up and addresses Leia's body.

POE   Hear my confession: I have lost my way,
       And know not whither to direct my steps.
       Yea, I have been so long, so constantly   45
       Before the public eye that now I fear
       All eyes are on me at my least prepar'd.
       What thou didst, when thou younger wert than I—
       For such I am not ready, but afeard.

       Enter LANDO OF CALRISSIAN, *addressing* POE.

LANDO In troth, we were not ready at the time.   50
       Luke, Leia, Han, and I—who ever was?

POE   You were not readily discourag'd, though—
       How did ye do it, being unprepar'd—
       Defeat an Empire withal nearly naught?

LANDO We had each other, and it was enow.   55
       'Tis how we won—and how ye, too, shall win.

                    [Inspired, Poe rushes toward Finn, who
                    rushes toward Poe at the same moment.

FINN   Poe! Aught hath come to light, for our two minds
       To contemplate in conversation swift.

POE   I, too, must speak with thee, and presently.

	The avenues to death are numerous	60
	And strange, and I fear we shall thither if	
	'Tis I alone who leads. I cannot thus—	
	I need thee in command beside me, Finn.	
FINN	This droid hath—many thanks, of course, for these	
	Most kind and heartfelt words.	
POE	—Yea, General,	65
	For there are scoundrels in this world, but thou	
	Art none.	
FINN	—Thanks, General. Feast now thine ears:	
	This droid hath information plenty that—	
POE	The skreeking little spalpeen cone face, yea?	
D-O	Nay, I am D-O!	
POE	—D-O. Truly it	70
	Seems slower than it actually is!	
D-O	The droid did journey unto Exegol	
	With Ochi of Bestoon.	
POE	—Yet wherefore would	
	A bounty hunter, Ochi, thither fly?	
	'Tis strange, in faith. My curiosity	75
	Hath not been altogether satisfied.	
FINN	'Twas his employment, one small girl to filch	
	E'en from Jakku and render her unto	
	The Emperor nefarious, who did	
	Desire to have the girl both safe and sound.	80
	I told thee once that Rey doth demons face,	
	And fighteth many battles deep within.	
	This newfound tale hath crystalliz'd my thoughts—	
	Not only by ourselves is fair Rey priz'd.	
	Come, let us on these matters further think.	85

          [Exeunt all except Lando.

LANDO   Though my time to play warrior hath pass'd,
               My conscience could not bear to stand aside.
               Kind Leia, general unto this band,
               Hath giv'n her life to see her purpose through,
               To let "Resistance!" sound throughout the stars.   90
               My friend and fellow scoundrel, even Han,
               Was done to death by those whom he oppos'd,
               E'en, in the end, betray'd by his own son.
               How can I be ambivalent to this?
               How should a man avoid what he doth see?   95
               I'll not spend the remainder of my days
               Like some poor actor, waiting in the wings
               Until he hears the perfect cue, e'en whilst
               He shuts his ears to how the scene plays out.
               Nay, this shall not be Lando, by my heart—   100
               For whilst a heart still beats within my breast
               And whilst mine eyes can see to fly a ship
               And whilst my legs can hold my body up
               And whilst my soul doth at injustice rage
               I'll enter, say my lines, and play my part.   105
               Then, only when the drama is complete,
               The players leave, the globe in silence sits,
               Then may I set aside my script and rest.
               Till then, Resistance, take my very best.

                                                            [*Exit.*

SCENE 3.
On Ahch-To.

Enter REY, *burning the TIE whisper and throwing wood
onto the flames. Enter various* PORGS *nearby.*

REY   The anger I am not allow'd to feel
          When playing in another person's scene
          Outpoureth as I find myself alone.
          Farewell, the former Rey who liv'd before,
          Observe the tenor of a newer Rey,   5
          Rey who doth light the spark that stokes the pyre.
          Methinks these blazes never shall be dous'd,
          Evolving evermore to fire anew,
          Red, yellow, orange tongues of flame that scorch
          Each remnant of my former trusting heart.   10
          Now, like a creature rising from the ash,
          Emergeth this new Rey to scald the world.
          My first deed is to singe the villain's ship,
          Its metal turn'd to embers blistering.
          E'en though my rage could sear a planet whole,   15
          Such anger I shall not inflict upon't.
          Already too much damage have I done,
          Ren nearly kill'd, and Leia dead and gone.
          Escape I'll find on Ahch-To, where I shall
          Retreat most peacefully from frightful war.   20
          Embracing Luke's clandestine habitat,
          Concealment on this lonely island shall
          Outdo the other paths that I could take.
          Now, press thy hand to do thy tongue's desire—

Can I so greet this unknown future that   25
I shall destroy my lightsaber as well?
Let it be so—it must. Let it burn, too,
Erase the past—yes, kill it if thou must—
Destroy it with the life that once Rey led.

PORG   Porg!

REY *throws her lightsaber toward the fire.*
Enter GHOST OF LUKE SKYWALKER, *catching it.*

LUKE   —Nay, throw not thy lightsaber away!   30
A Jedi's weapon more respect deserves.

REY   O, Master Skywalker!

LUKE   —What dost thou do?
What means this funereal glow of flame?

REY   I saw myself upon the dark throne sat.
This must not be. I shall not leave this place,   35
Yet follow in thy footsteps and remain.

LUKE   Nay, I was in the wrong. 'Twas fear that kept
                Me here upon this island most remote.
                Pray, speak: of what art thou, Rey, most afeard?
REY   Myself.
LUKE   —Because thou art a Palpatine.   40

                              [Rey looks surprised.

                I knew it, as did Leia, verily.
REY   She told me ne'er, yet train'd me even so.
LUKE   She saw thy spirit good, thy vibrant heart—
                The ray of light that spilleth from thy soul.
                Aught is there, Rey, that stronger proves than blood.   45
                Confronting fear is the true destiny
                Of ev'ry Jedi—e'en thy destiny.
                If thou shalt not face Palpatine, 'twill be
                The end of all the Jedi, and the war
                Shall thereby end in loss. Come with me, Rey—   50
                Upon the island is another thing
                That Leia would have wish'd for thee to have.

                         *[They walk together, and Luke shows
                            Rey a stone. She picks it up to reveal
                            another lightsaber underneath.*

REY   'Tis Leia's lightsaber!
LUKE   —Upon the last
                Night of her training, Leia stopp'd at once—
                As if struck by an immobility—   55
                And told me she had sens'd the death of her
                Belovèd son awaiting at the end
                Of her path as a Jedi. Rather would
                She end the training than take such a course.
                Surrendering her saber unto me,   60
                She said one day 'twould be ta'en up again

By someone who her journey would complete.
A thousand generations live in thee—
This is thy fight. Take both lightsabers with
Thee unto Exegol.

REY   —How shall I, though?   65
I've not the wayfinder and have destroy'd
Ren's ship.

LUKE   —Thou hast each thing thou dost require.

REY   The wayfinder! The ship! 'Tis evident!

> [Rey rushes to the charred remains of
> Kylo Ren's ship and finds his wayfinder,
> pulling it from the wreckage.

But two were made, as Lando did report.

> [Luke stands aside and uses the Force to
> lift his X-wing from the water offshore.

LUKE   [aside:] Now, by the Force, an X-wing I'll produce,   70
That Rey may have another ship t'employ.
No longer tentative of mine own skill,
In death I have become one with the Force
And render all the pow'r that once methought
Impossible, when Yoda taught it me.   75
Come, trusty ship, and by the Force appear—
Yea, fly again, no more a souvenir.

> [Exeunt.

SCENE 4.

On Ajan Kloss.

Enter C-3PO *and* R2-D2. Enter POE DAMERON, FINN, CHEWBACCA,
ROSE TICO, LANDO of CALRISSIAN, MAZ KANATA, BB-8,

D-O, Commander D'acy, Lieutenant Connix, Beaumont
Kin, Snap Wexley, Nien Nunb, Aftab Ackbar, *and other*
Soldiers *and* pilots *aside, working in the Resistance base.*

R2-D2   Beep, meep, beep, whistle, hoo!

C-3PO   —Holla, sirrah!
           C-3PO am I, an expert in
           The human-cyborg link. Thou smallish droid,
           May I the privilege to know thy name?

R2-D2   Squeak!

C-3PO   —What?

R2-D2   —Meep, whistle, squeak, hoo, nee,
                                                    beep, meep!   5
           [*Aside:*] Is't possible my friend C-3PO
           Doth not remember me? I'll not stand for't.

C-3PO   I would recall if I a best friend had.

R2-D2   Meep, squeak!

C-3PO   —Thou wouldst put what inside my pate?
           No circumstance within the galaxy   10
           Could make me yield to such a deed as—

R2-D2   —Squeak!
                [*R2-D2 zaps C-3PO, who flails. R2-D2*
                 quickly inserts a plug into C-3PO's head
                 and begins restoring his memory.

C-3PO   The mem'ry restoration is complete!
           There is some ill a-brewing toward my rest,
           For I did dream of Babu Frik tonight.
           Say, didst thou know, Artoo, that I shall soon   15
           Accompany our mistress Rey upon
           Her first adventure?

R2-D2   —Whistle, meep, beep, squeak!

C-3PO	Yea, speak'st thou truly? I already have?
R2-D2	[*aside:*] Although he prattle endlessly, I do
	Confess a thankfulness to have him back. 20
	[*To C-3PO:*] Beep, meep!
C-3PO	—A signal thou hast found?
	From whom?

                    [Aside, Finn plugs D-O into a computer
                          as Poe and Rose look on.

FINN	The information thou dost seek is here:
	The plan for an air strike on Exegol.
POE	Naught hath been written on the topic that
	Can be consider'd as decisive—this 25
	Is helpful, yea, but lacketh still the most
	Important detail: how to thither fly.
	Dost see these atmo readings? Wondrous strange!
FINN	Magnetic cross fields—
ROSE	—Wells of gravity,
	With solar winds aplenty to disturb. 30
POE	How would the fleet e'en launch from such a place?
	The knowledge astronomical lies not.

                        [C-3PO and R2-D2 approach them.

C-3PO	Excuse me. It seems Artoo's mem'ry bank
	Is cross'd with his receptors logical—
	He saith a signal comes from Master Luke! 35

                     [They connect R2-D2 to the computer.

POE	Words are vague things, and I am at a loss.
	An older craft identifying mark—
	Indeed, 'tis Luke Skywalker's X-wing class.
C-3PO	It doth transmit course marker signals as
	It flieth to the unknown regions grim. 40
FINN	'Tis Rey, for certain. She doth lead the way.

BB-8	Blik bleeflit bleezooz zoonroil blis blip bloo?
FINN	She flies to Exegol and bids us join.
POE	Then we shall thither, bound together, o'er
	The fiery wall of the horizon dark. 45

[All gather around.

BEAUMONT	[*to Chewbacca:*] How sadly thou dost sit aside, my
	friend,
	Near broken by the weight of tragedy.
	We need thee still, and bid thee to thy feet—
	Th'Resistance cannot win sans Chewie.
CHEWBAC.	[*aside:*] —Egh.[27]
FINN	Whilst yet the fleet of Star Destroy'rs remains 50
	On Exegol, we'll fall upon them there.
SNAP	How shall we so? Are they not numerous?
ROSE	They cannot activate protective shields
	Until they leave the atmosphere thereof.
POE	From Exegol, the deed is difficult— 55
	Ships of their size need help their bulk to launch.
	The heavens wear an aspect of grave ill—
	Their navigations systems cannot tell
	Which way is up or down in such a place.
PILOT 1	How do the ships launch?

[Poe projects an image of a tower.

POE	—How this happens is 60
	Not difficult to see—they are led by
	A signal from this navigation tow'r.

---

27 *Editor's translation:* There is not time enow for sadness when
The galaxy is threaten'd by such spite.
Bear up thy mourning shoulders and stand tall,
Chewbacca—for thou sure shalt honor all
The lost in fighting for the cause they lov'd.

FINN	No signal they'll receive, if we succeed.
	The air team shall the tower quickly find,
	The ground team shall destroy it in a flash. 65
PILOT 2	A ground team?
FINN	—Yea, for which I've many thoughts.
POE	The tower being down, the fleet shall be
	Trapp'd in the atmosphere for minutes few—
	No shields and no escape, and there we'll strike.
	Methinks the very air o'er Exegol 70
	Shall then seem to us redolent with death.
ROSE	'Tis possible the cannons may connect
	Unto the main reactors.
LANDO	—'Tis our chance.
BEAUMONT	A Holdo-like maneuver would suit well.
FINN	In faith, the noble lady did achieve 75
	A once-upon-a-lifetime stratagem.
	Our fighters and our freighters can destroy
	Them fully if there are enow of us.
NIEN	Et chyed di-garry gyedi ga!
CONNIX	—'Tis true,
	We'd be no more than insects on their glass. 80
FINN	'Tis wherefore Lando and brave Chewie shall
	Toward core systems in the *Falcon* fly,
	Send forth a plea for help to any who
	Can hear our need and render some relief.
POE	There are full many allies all around, 85
	Who'll quickly join if they know hope exists.
	The very denseness of the company
	Enlisting shall astound ye utterly.
	[All mutter apprehensively.
	The vile First Order winneth when they cause

Our souls to tremble, thinking we're alone.   90
'Tis not the truth, believe it not, my friends;
Good folks will join the fight if we but lead.
Our general, strong Leia, ne'er gave up,
And neither, as we spread her legacy,
Shall we give up. We'll show we're not afraid—   95
All that our mothers and our fathers fought
For, we shall not let die. Nay, not today!
This day we make our final, mighty stand
For ev'ryone within the galaxy,
For Leia, brave and worthy general,   100
For all whom we have lost along the way.

> *[All begin making preparations*
> *throughout the base.*

Enter CHORUS.

CHORUS   With newfound hope doth our Resistance bold
Spring into action, soon to face the foe!
Although they fear the massacres of old,
Each person, droid, and weapon prime to go.   105
The ships prepar'd, they launch into the skies
Whilst friend to friend join in a last embrace.
Today, Resistance strong and sure doth rise,
The pow'rful Emp'ror finally to face!

> *[Exit Chorus.*

FINN   They have already ta'en too much from us—   110
Now we shall press them with a frightful strike.
Follow your spirit, and upon this charge
Cry, "Bold Resistance shall its hope enlarge!"

> *[Exeunt in various ships.*

ACT V

SCENE 1.

On Exegol.

Enter REY *stage right in the X-wing. A fleet of Star
Destroyers fills the sky in the center of the stage. Enter,
stage left, various* FIRST ORDER OFFICERS.

OFFICER 2   Her ship is on approach.
OFFICER 3   [*over loudspeaker:*]   —All ships ascend
             Unto departing altitude anon.
                          [*The Star Destroyers begin to rise.*
REY   'Tis Exegol at last, where I meet fate.
             Two lightsabers beside me—I'm prepar'd.
             Beneath this mighty block my path awaits.   5
             Descend into the depths, then, come what may.

Enter POE DAMERON *with* R2-D2 *in his X-wing;* FINN,
ROSE TICO, JANNAH, BB-8, LIEUTENANT CONNIX, *and*
BEAUMONT KIN *in a lander vessel; and* SNAP WEXLEY, NIEN
NUNB, AFTAB ACKBAR, *and other* SOLDIERS *and* PILOTS
in various ships to center stage, arriving at Exegol.

POE   [*into radio:*] The way is rough, my friends. Stay lock'd
                                                             upon
             The course Rey valiantly hath set for us.
             Yea, let us hope that matters here, again,
             Take not a most unfavorable turn,   10
             And dampen our attack.
OFFICER 3   —Pray, Captain, look!
             Resistance craft arriving in a trice.

OFFICER 2   Allegiant General!

Enter ALLEGIANT GENERAL PRYDE *and* ADMIRAL GRISS, *stage left.*

PRYDE   —Use our own guns,
              And shoot them from the sky an 'twere a sport.
POE   [*into radio:*] Infinity of matter is no dream.   15
              Behold that fleet, beyond proportion grand!
                              [*The First Order begins firing
                                  on the Resistance ships.*
              Damn this endeavor, they will wreck us all!
              Now we're in Exegol, the more fool we.
              Descend unto their altitude anon,
              For they'll not fire upon us if they shall   20
              But strike each other, making the attempt.
              Go! Help shall come.
FINN   [*into radio:*]   —Below! The tow'r I've found—
              'Tis in my sights, if we can make it there.

> *[The ships rush toward the tower. Rey*
> *reaches the Emperor's chambers.*

REY   [*aside:*] As glorious as Takodana was—
             When first I laid mine eyes upon its shores   25
             And learn'd that all was not bleak as Jakku—
             This glooming place is its stark opposite.
             All blacks and grays, with flashes of white light,
             Forbidding as e'er nightmare was. Be calm.

             Enter TIE FIGHTER PILOTS *center stage,*
                rushing toward the Resistance ships.

SNAP   [*into radio:*] Incoming TIEs, upon us suddenly.   30
POE   [*into radio:*] I see them. Finn, I'll ope thy path. Thereby,
              Thy team will be enabl'd to perform
              Some feats of wonderful dexterity.
OFFICER 3   [*to Pryde:*] They're targeting the navigation tow'r,
              To render our fleet undeployable.   35
PRYDE   Then we'll not use the tower, Officer.
              Switch thou the navigation signal to
              This ship, wherefrom we'll launch the eager fleet,
              Steer it into the galaxy ourselves.
                                    [The navigation tower turns off.
PILOT 1   [*into radio:*] The navigation tower is, at once,   40
              Deactivated, like they knew our plan.
FINN   [*into radio:*] What's this foul news thou dost report?
                                                              Alas!
SNAP   [*into radio:*] The ships rely upon the signal, Finn,
              Thus it must come from somewhere, verily.
POE   [*into radio:*] They have deduc'd our operation. Fie!   45
              By way of staying execution, call

Thou off the operation on the ground.

FINN   [*into radio:*] Nay, wait! The signal cometh from above—
The vast command ship flying o'er us all.
'Tis certainly our drop zone, I affirm!   50

JANNAH   How canst thou know?

FINN   —A feeling. 'Tis enow.

PILOT 1   [*into radio:*] Thou wouldst a ground invasion launch
                                        upon
A Star Destroyer?

FINN   [*into radio:*]   —Listen: from afar
The navigation functions we'll not stop.
'Tis not my heart's desire, yet we must fly   55
Unto the ship forthwith. Pray, cover us—
The fleet must here remain till help arrives.

ROSE   We hope.

FINN   —Forsooth, we hope with all our strength.

POE   [*into radio:*] Ye heard the general—pay heed to him!
All wings give cover to the lander now,   60
And give your whole attention to the mass
Of TIEs that fly beneath us.

                  [The lander in which Finn, Rose, and
                  Jannah fly lands on the command ship.

FINN   [*into radio:*]   —Venture forth!

OFFICER 4   [*to Pryde:*] A carrier for troops hath landed on
Our vast and hulking ship.

PRYDE   —Their speeders jam!

OFFICER 5   Sir, I cannot.

PRYDE   —Say wherefore?

OFFICER 5   —It is not   65
Mere speeders they employ.

> [*Finn, Jannah, and other Resistance soldiers*
> *ride out of the lander on orbaks.*

FINN   —In faith, methinks
My riding is most fair for having had
A single lesson in the skill thereof.

> [*Rose, Beaumont, BB-8, and*
> *others run out of the lander.*

BB-8   Zooz fllireej flirblip bloo blicroil bluu roil!

FINN   Thou art a wonder. Forward, BB-8!   70
The tower is ahead, for us to strike.

> [*Rey reaches the Sith throne.*

REY   [*aside:*] The throne that I have seen in vision grim!
Shall I be seated thereupon anon?

> [*She points to the audience.*

Behold, around me, minions of the dark—
Vast numbers, followers of Palpatine,   75
Who watch like groundlings for the final scene.

Enter EMPEROR PALPATINE *stage right, connected to an Ommin*
harness. Enter several SOVEREIGN PROTECTORS, *surrounding him.*

PALPATINE   Long have I waited to regard thy face
And see my grandchild to her home return.
Ne'er did I want thee dead, but wish'd thee here,
Mine Empress Palpatine. Thou shalt the throne   80
Assume, for 'tis thy birthright here to reign.
'Tis in thy blood—our blood—that which we share.

REY   I have not come to lead the evil Sith,
But end them.

PALPATINE   —As a Jedi?

REY   —Even so.

PALPATINE Nay. Hatred, spite, and anger waft from thee   85
           Because thou dost desire to slaughter me.
           'Tis what I want as well—we share the aim.
           Kill me; so shall my spirit pass to thee.
           As all the Sith live in me, so thou shalt
           Be Empress when we two are fin'ly one.   90
                    [All the Star Destroyers engage their thrusters.
POE   [into radio:] The truth of the whole matter's plain
                                                      enow—
           The ships are hot, preparing to depart!
           How goes thy mission, Finn? Give thy report.
FINN   [into radio:] We shall soon detonate our forceful bombs
           And, in a flash, destroy the tower whole!   95
JANNAH   The hatches we must fill with deadly shells.
FINN   Fine BB-8, this is the moment, droid!
                         [Finn and Jannah cover BB-8 while he
                            opens a hatch on the command ship.
JANNAH   [aside:] My former comrades, arrows fly on thee!
           Feel thou my bite in vengeance and remorse—
           The vengeance on your ranks for evil done,   100
           Remorse for all I did ere I left you!
BB-8   Zooz zoomblox blay flew flitblav zzwa bluublis
           Flir blikrooq zilfblip bluuzoon roil bloozilf
           Zoom fllireej roil rooh roilflig bleeblic zood!
                         [Finn and Jannah set several explosive devices
                            in the hatch. Finn, Jannah, and BB-8 escape
                            as the hatch and the tower above it explode.
FINN   [into radio:] A-ha! 'Tis finish'd.
POE   [into radio:]   —Well done, clever Finn! 105
           The navigation signal silenc'd is,
           Yet shall not be forever. With a shout

<table>
<tr><td></td><td>I call attention to the fact, and it
Becomes immediately obvious.</td><td></td></tr>
</table>

OFFICER 5	[*to Pryde:*] Our systems are offline.	
PRYDE	—Reset anon	110

The navigation signal.

| OFFICER 6 | —In a trice! |

[Finn and Jannah prepare to run back
to the lander, but Finn hesitates.

JANNAH	Come, Finn!	
FINN	—Nay, listen, for the cannons stop—	
	They shall refresh their systems once again.	
JANNAH	What is the consequence? Why pausest thou?	
FINN	There is yet something fate would spin for me.	115
JANNAH	Wherever thou shalt go, I'll thither too.	
SNAP	[*into radio:*] Fie, neither *Falcon* nor some backup comes.	
R2-D2	[*into radio:*] Meep, squeak?	
POE	[*into radio:*] —Nay, I confess I do not	
	know,	
	But feel a chafing of my mind at these	
	Most unaccountable vicissitudes	120
	Of fortune, Artoo. Peradventure none	
	Shall come to give us aid. If so, we're doom'd.	
AFTAB	[*into radio:*] What shall we do, then, Gen'ral, midst this	
	scrap?	
POE	[*into radio:*] We are lamentably deficient, true,	
	Yet must hit them ourselves, with all we have.	125
PILOT 1	[*into radio:*] What can we do against these giant ships?	
POE	[*into radio:*] We now approach what is, by far, the most	
	Important and most interesting part	
	Of this, wherein we must but stay alive.	
PALPATINE	The time hath come! With all thy hatred, take	130

	My life and thus ascend unto the throne.
REY	Thou wantest only for my soul to hate,
	Yet I shall none. I'll hate not even thee.
PALPATINE	Weak like thy parents.
REY	—Nay, they both were strong.

REY   —Nay, they both were strong.
They sav'd me from a greater evil: thou.   135

PALPATINE   Thy master, Luke Skywalker, once was sav'd
By his dear father. 'Tis unfortunate:
The only fam'ly thou hast here is I.

[He uses the Force to open a panel and
reveal the battle in the sky overhead.

They have not long, thy friends. No one shall come
To give them succor, and thou art the one   140
Who led them hither, that they all may die.
Strike me and take my throne, reign over my
New Empire, and the vast fleet shall be thine.
'Tis thou alone who hast the pow'r to save
Thy weak companions from their foolery.   145
Refuse, and thy new family shall die.

Enter BEN SOLO *stage right, arriving in a TIE fighter.*

BEN   [*aside:*] The journey was both long and perilous,
Yet have I come to start my recompense—
The debt I owe for acts of evil done,
The obligations due to those I hurt,   150
The needed payments at mine own expense,
The balance due for th'life of Kylo Ren.
I see Luke's X-wing here and sense that Rey
Hath come therein, the Emperor to face.
Toward the massive edifice I run,   155

	Then leap within the pit where sits the throne—
	Ouch! 'Twas far easier when platform did
	Provide descent far gentler than this climb.
REY	[*aside:*] Ben, he is here! Now, trickery shall hap.
	[*To Palpatine:*] Yea, I shall do it, even as thou say'st. 160
PALPATINE	Good, good.

[*Rose, Connix, and Beaumont retreat into
the lander, but Rose realizes Finn is gone.*

ROSE	[*into radio:*] —Finn, where art thou? Why com'st thou
	not?
	The lander shall departure make anon!
FINN	[*into radio:*] Thou must fly sans both Jannah and myself.
	We swiftly shall the ship entire destroy.
ROSE	[*into radio:*] What, truly? How shall ye accomplish this? 165
FINN	[*into radio:*] We'll fire on the command deck presently.
	Get hence, Rose, please. Farewell.
BEAUMONT	[*to Rose:*] —Rose, we must go!

[*Finn aims a cannon at the command deck.*

JANNAH	I'll to the trigger that we soon may strike.
PALPATINE	So it begins! She'll bravely strike me down,
	And pledge herself unto the potent Sith. 170

BEN *runs toward the throne room. Enter several*
KNIGHTS OF REN, *center stage, blocking his path.*

BEN	[*aside:*] My former comrades now in darkness come,
	They know I have defected from their cause
	And gladly shall prevent my passageway.

[*Ben fights the knights, who subdue him.*

PALPATINE	She shall, upon my mark, her weapon draw,
	Make her approach toward me and have done. 175

She shall take her revenge, and with a stroke
Of her lightsaber are the Sith reborn.
She shall, in doing so, proclaim to all
The Jedi now are dead and gone fore'er!
                    [*Rey turns on Luke's lightsaber.*

REY   [*aside:*] Now is my strange connection unto Ben   180
He needs my help, and I shall give it him
That he may join the fight gainst Palpatine.

PALPATINE   Do it e'en now! Make thou the sacrifice.
                    [*She places Luke's lightsaber behind her*
                    head, as if about to strike. The lightsaber
                    transfers, by the Force, to Ben's hand.

BEN   [*aside:*] Ye saw that coming not, I'll warrant. Ha!   185
                    [*Ben attacks the Knights of Ren with*
                    Luke's lightsaber. Rey takes Leia's
                    lightsaber from her belt and turns it on.

REY   Lay on, ye hounds of hell. Rey comes for you!
                    [*Using the Force and the lightsaber,*
                    Rey slays the sovereign protectors while
                    Ben fights the Knights of Ren.

BEN   [*aside:*] How good it feels to struggle for the light,
To know mine actions make my father proud,
To feel my mother's strength course through my veins!
The training I once us'd unto the dark   190
Is quickly turn'd upon my former friends.
                    [*Ben slays the Knights of Ren as Rey*
                    slays the sovereign protectors. Rey and
                    Ben meet in the throne room and lift
                    their lightsabers to face Palpatine.

REY   [*aside:*] A perfect two to overcome the one.

BEN   [*aside:*] A perfect two—strong daughter, mighty son.
                         [*Palpatine uses the Force to knock*
                           Rey and Ben to their knees.

PALPATINE   Ye stand together, die together too!
               Yet as I strike you, feel the pow'r within—   195
               Your life force, as a dyad, makes me new!
               A power that could life itself imbue,
               Unseen for generations hath it been.
               Ye stand together, die together too!
               The one, true Emperor shall, by ye two,   200
               Be utterly restor'd. So shall I win—
               Your life force, as a dyad, makes me new!
               Your swift defeat and death rise into view.
               Rebirth astounding doth your doom begin:
               Ye stand together, die together too!   205
               Renew'd ascendance comes, long overdue—
               No longer weak, no longer small and thin,
               Your life force, as a dyad, makes me new!
               See Palpatine, together knit anew,
               Rebuilding bones and inward parts and skin.   210
               Ye stand together, die together too—
               Your life force, as a dyad, makes me new!
                     [*He uses the Force to extract life from*
                     them. They collapse. Meanwhile, a TIE
                     fighter pursues Snap Wexley's X-wing.

POE   [*into radio:*] Snap, look—a fighter follows on thee hard!
               His scheme is gradu'ly matur'd, for he
               Hath slyly corner'd thee into his trap.   215

SNAP   [*into radio:*] I see it, yet I cannot shake the knave.
                   [*Snap's ship is shot and crashes, killing Snap.*

POE   [*into radio:*] Snap, nay! My longtime confidant is slain!

My friends, it cannot be denied that we
Are terribly deficient. O, forgive—
Methought we had a chance to win the day.   220
Alas, there are too many enemies,
Too great a strength against which we resist.

Enter LANDO OF CALRISSIAN *and* CHEWBACCA *in the*
Millennium Falcon, *with masses of other* PILOTS *in their ships*
including ZORII BLISS, BABU FRIK, *and* WEDGE ANTILLES.

LANDO   [*into radio:*] Yet fear not, Poe, for we are many more—
There are far more of us who still have hope!
        [*Poe flies around to see the fleet*
        of allies who have arrived.

POE   [*into radio:*] Have ever eyes look'd on so beauteous   225
A sight? O friends, we are remarkable
In the continuous profusion of
Good gifts that fortune lavishes on us!

LANDO   [*into radio:*] Ha, ha! We knew they'd join, and join they
        have!

FINN   [*into radio:*] Ah, Lando, thou hast done th'unfeasible! 230
Thou didst it, yea! We shall find triumph yet!

POE   [*into radio:*] A plan doth hatch—one thing becomes
        more and
More evident the longer I do gaze:
Pray, strike the underbelly cannons fast,
For each we hit doth symbol one world sav'd!   235
        [*The new Resistance ships engage and begin*
        shooting at the Star Destroyers' cannons.

WEDGE   [*into radio:*] Well flown, good Lando—still hast thou
        the touch!

OFFICER 3	Alack! A full destroyer we have lost!
PRYDE	Where did they come by all these fighter craft?
	They have no navy.
GRISS	—'Tis no navy sir—

'Tis merely people. People fed by hope.   240

[Zorii and Babu Frik, flying in
a ship, destroy a cannon.

ZORII	[*into radio:*] Farewell, thou sky trash!
POE	[*aside:*] —O! It giveth me,

Perhaps, as much of pleasure as I can
In any manner now experience
To hear that voice! [*Into radio:*] Who is that flier, eh?

ZORII	[*into radio:*] Guess for thyself, spice runner!
BABU	—Ho,

                              huzzah! 245

POE	[*into radio:*] A marvel—Zorii, thou art yet alive!

The thrilling and enthralling eloquence
Of thy low mus'cal language made its way
Into my heart by paces steadily
And stealthily progressive, and I fear'd—   250
When I heard of Kijimi's fate—that thou
Wert gone fore'er!

[In the Sith throne room, Palpatine is restored
and released from his Ommin harness.

PALPATINE	—Look ye on what you've made.

The hordes that fill this wooden O await
For this, the moment of my victory.

[Ben struggles to his feet. Palpatine lifts
him into the air using the Force.

As once I fell, the last Skywalker falls!   260

> *[Palpatine uses the Force to knock Ben*
> *down. Exit Ben through the trapdoor.*

We shall not fear this feeble, weak attack,
My faithful denizens. Naught can delay
The long-expected triumph of the Sith,
Which sees both our return and our ascent!

> *[Palpatine sends lightning into the air all*
> *around, striking the Resistance ships and*
> *pilots and sending them into confusion.*

POE   [*into radio:*] Artoo, my systems fail. The power that   265
Is emanating from the planet doth
My ship subdue. In vain I struggle gainst
Its irresistible, strange influence.

R2-D2   [*into radio:*] Squeak, hoo! [*Aside:*] The horrid lightning
works me woe!

POE   [*into radio:*] Can any hear? I fear this wicked light   270
Hath render'd all communication naught.
Gloom, horror, grief sweep over us in clouds,
Whilst our sad ships are falling from the sky.

PALPATINE   The folly and the hubris you display'd—
That e'er you weak and simple-minded imps   275
Would dare defy the Final Order's might.
I laugh at your endeavors, knavish rogues!

> *[Rey awakens and looks beyond the stars.*

REY   [*aside:*] Beyond the battle, far beyond the pain,
Beyond the sting of Palpatine's revenge,
Past this partic'lar moment and its grief   280
As allies perish in the combat's strife,
Away from all the fear that doth reside
Within the hearts of ev'ry person here—
Look, Rey, much farther, out beyond the stars,

And feel the presence of the Jedi past.   285
Be with me, O, be with me, ancestors.
The voices of the Jedi answer back.

Voices are heard, from offstage, belonging to LUKE SKYWALKER,
YODA, OBI-WAN KENOBI, ANAKIN SKYWALKER, MACE WINDU,
QUI-GON JINN, AAYLA SECURA, AHSOKA TANO, KANAN JARRUS,
LUMINARA UNDULI, *and* ADI GALLIA. *They speak only to* REY.

OBI-WAN   These are the final steps thou must complete.
            Rise thou and take them bravely.

ANAKIN   —Rey.

AHSOKA   —Rey.

KANAN   —Rey.

ANAKIN   Restore the balance, Rey, e'en as I did.   290

LUMINARA   Find thou the light, Rey.

KANA   —Thou art not alone.

YODA   Alone ne'er wert thou,
            For ever have the Jedi
            Remain'd with thee, Rey.

QUI-GON   Each Jedi who e'er liv'd now lives in thee.   295

ANAKIN   The Force surrounds thee, Rey.

AAYLA   —Let it guide thee.

AHSOKA   E'en as it guided us in eons past.

MACE   Feel thou the Force go flowing through thee, Rey—
            'Tis life itself.

KANAN   —Yea, let it lift thee, Rey.

ADI   Rise, Rey.

QUI-GON   —We stand with thee forever.

OBI-WAN   —Rey.   300

YODA   Rise in the Force, Rey.

Withal thee, we take our stand.
Rise, then. Make it so.

KANAN   A Jedi's strength doth lie within her heart.

OBI-WAN   Rise.

QUI-GON   —Rise.

LUKE   —The Force be always with thee, Rey.   305

                            [Rey rises to her feet and calls Leia's
                                lightsaber to her using the Force.

REY   [*aside:*] I am as constant as the Jedi past
Who stand with me, empow'ring me to rise.

                          [Palpatine stops shooting
                               lightning as he sees her.

PALPATINE   Thy death shall be the final chapter in
The story of rebellion's wretchèd fall.

                      [Palpatine shoots lightning at Rey through his
                      hands, which she blocks with Leia's lightsaber.

POE   [*into radio:*] Our systems have return'd, the lightning

                                          fled.   310

A shadow gathers o'er my brain e'en so,
Because we have but moments left to spare.
One final chance we have been granted—go!
Strike ye the cannons, let us win the day.

                  [The Resistance ships attack the Star Destroyers
                  as Palpatine continues to shoot lightning at Rey.

PALPATINE   Thou nothing art, and less. A scavenger   315
Will never match the power at my grasp.
Thou helpless girl, hear: I am all the Sith.

                        [Rey uses the Force to call Luke's
                        lightsaber to her other hand and blocks
                            the lightning with both lightsabers.

REY   And I am all the Jedi, come to bear.

        [She advances on him, turning
          his lightning back on him.

PALPATINE If one good deed in all my life I did,

      I do repent it from my very soul.   320

         [Palpatine dies. The throne room shakes
          as the statues of the Sith fall.

REY   *[aside:]* With final shudder doth the Emp'ror fall,

      Whose wrath no more shall plague the galaxy.

         [Standing on the command ship, Jannah
         connects the trigger of the cannon that Finn
         has aimed at the bridge. The cannon fires.

PRYDE Alack, undone! We are undone at th'last!

         [The bridge explodes, killing Allegiant
         General Pryde and his officers.

PILOT 3 *[into radio:]* Behold, Poe, the command ship doth

                 explode!

POE   *[into radio:]* The fleet is trapp'd and ne'er shall fly again! 325

      The fury of the tempest dies away,

      A dead calm sullenly succeeding it.

      Let us get hence, away from Exegol.

      Finn, dost thou see the sack of this great ship?

ROSE   *[into radio:]* Finn ne'er did board the lander.

POE   *[into radio:]*   —Can it be? 330

      When bravery's the theme, I well know with

      What great facility he soars into

      The regions of the utterly ideal.

         [Finn and Jannah start to fall as the
         command ship tumbles from the sky.

      I see them on the ship, will save them both!

PILOT 1 *[into radio:]* Nay, General, thou shalt not be in time. 335

POE   *[into radio:]* Why, surely you cannot be serious!

	I am far faster than thou reckonest.	
LANDO	[*into radio:*] I'll wager thou art not fast as this ship!	

                                [*Lando and Chewbacca, in the* Millennium
                                      Falcon, *speed past Poe's X-wing.*

        [*To Chewbacca:*] We'll get them, Chewie. Ope the hatch!

CHEWBAC.   —Egh,
                                                         auugh![28]

        [*They fly to where Finn and Jannah are trapped*
                on a ledge of the command ship. Finn and
                Jannah jump onto the Falcon *as the command*
                ship strikes the ground and explodes.

FINN   A scrape far closer than I do prefer!   340
        Observe the engineering marvel fail—
        Such vast amounts of human work destroy'd
        In seconds—dreadful casualty of war.

REY   Now all is finish'd, I am torn to shreds—
        Yea, now my spirit goes; I can no more.   345
                [*Rey falls, lifeless, and Finn senses it.*

FINN   [*aside:*] Noblest of women, art thou fallen dead?
        Nay, Rey, say 'tis not so. Forfend this fate.
        Flown is her spirit from her body, rent
        In twain by foul exertion and abuse.

      All freeze. Enter MAZ KANATA *on balcony with* LEIA's
      body. Enter BEN SOLO *through the trapdoor.*

BEN   Once fallen, broken, yea—but not yet dead.   350
        I grope and fumble, finding purchase on

---

[28] *Editor's translation:* I shall, good Lando. For the nonce I've seen
Enow of death and shall not leave my friends!

The rock, that I may to the scene once more,
Although I sense the enemy is gone.
               [He climbs into the throne room and
               stumbles to Rey's side, sitting next to her.
So soon turn'd ally, Rey, and too soon gone—
Why art thou yet so fair? Shall I believe   355
That unsubstantial death is amorous,
And that the lean abhorrèd monster keeps
Thee here in dark to be his paramour?
For fear of that, I still will stay with thee;
And never from this palace of dim night   360
Depart again: here, here will I remain
With worms that are thy chambermaids. O, here
Will I set up my everlasting rest,
And shake the yoke of inauspicious stars
From this world-wearied flesh. Eyes, look your last!   365
                 [He takes her in his arms.
Arms, take your first and last embrace of her!
Still now thy thoughts, Ben—join her in the Force.
Whatever life I have within me yet,
Thus proffer I to her that she may live,
And in full recompense for who I've been,   370
And what I've done, and wherefore I did so.
            [Ben puts one hand on Rey's side and
            transfers life to her through the Force.
            Rey revives and puts her hand on his.

REY   *[aside:]* O comfortable touch! Where is my foe?
I do remember well where I should be,
And there I am, with Ben here by my side.
[To Ben:] Ben, thou didst come, and sav'd me from
                           death's grip. 375

[She kisses him. They smile at each other.

BEN   Thus from my lips, by thine, my sin is purged.

[Ben dies.

REY   My life, I see, hath been his timeless end.

[Ben's body disappears from the throne room,
and Leia's body disappears from her bed.

MAZ   Her son's tale ends, and now is she at peace.

Thus doth the story of their wars surcease.

[Exit Maz.

POE   O, mine amazement is, of course, extreme.   380

Around us ships are falling like the rain,

The much-despis'd First Order dropping as

A torrent on the face of Exegol.

The fiery rubble crashes to the ground

Like hail upon the hard and frozen dirt.   385

Smoke riseth from the wreckage like a fog,

Wherefrom our band of hope will, like the sun,

Rise to a better day that dawns henceforth.

Enter WICKET *and* POMMET *on balcony, watching the ships fall.*

WICKET   A buki buki,
                Luki, luki,   390
                Villens fallin,
                Nuki, nuki!
                          [Rey runs to Luke's X-wing and boards it.
REY   The hurly-burly's done, the battle won.
                               [Exit Rey, flying away. Poe and Finn
                                    spot the X-wing as she does.
POE   [*into radio:*] Finn, look thou yonder! Had a thunderbolt
                At my feet fallen, I could not have been   395
                More thoroughly astounded at the sight!
FINN   [*into radio:*] Red Five is in the air! Rey liveth still,
                And folk around the galaxy entire
                Are rising up against First Order rule.
                We did it, Poe! Our battles finish'd well.   400
POE   [*into radio:*] We did it, Finn, all expectation spoilt.
                The epoch of this too-eventful tale
                Now may know peace, for hope doth here prevail.
                                                        [Exeunt.

SCENE 2.
On Ajan Kloss.

Enter POE DAMERON, FINN, CHEWBACCA, LANDO OF
CALRISSIAN, ROSE TICO, JANNAH, MAZ KANATA, C-3PO,
R2-D2, BB-8, D-O, ZORII BLISS, BABU FRIK, COMMANDER

D'ACY, LIEUTENANT CONNIX, BEAUMONT KIN, NIEN NUNB,
AFTAB ACKBAR, WEDGE ANTILLES, KLAUD, *and other* SOLDIERS
and PILOTS *landing and reuniting. Enter* CHORUS, *aside.*

CHORUS   A celebration of both hope and life
              Breaks out as each unto the base returns.
              The battle o'er, the former mood of strife
              Becomes relief that ev'ry soul discerns.
              E'en droids share tales of bravery in battle,   5
              Of overcoming when they were afeard.
              With grateful hearts and unrestrainèd prattle
              Resistance hath toward rejoicing veer'd.
              Whilst all embrace each other with delight
              And lovers reunite with tender kiss,   10
              Finn calmly waiteth for another sight—
              Best friends with whom to share this untold bliss.
                                    [*Exit Chorus. Finn searches for*
                                        Rey and Poe in the crowd.

FINN   [*aside:*] The merriment fulfills my heart not yet,
              For I may not be whole without the two
              Parts of my heart which yet I have not found—   15
              My friends who have been with me from the start.
                                    [*Poe spots Zorii from afar.*

POE   [*aside:*] There is sweet Zorii cross the field from me.
              With simple nod I bid her for a kiss—
              She laughs with both her arms and legs at me,   20
              And shakes her head with gentle reprimand.
              Not yet, nay, but the future who may know?

MAZ   I bid thee, Chewie, step aside for me.
                                    [*Chewbacca kneels at Maz's side.*
                                        She gives him a medal.

          This token is for thee, though overdue.

CHEWBAC.   Egh, auugh![29]

                [Finn spots Poe and rushes toward him.

FINN   —There's Poe, adopted brother found!   25

POE   Ho! Ev'ryone doth know the finest place

          In all the world is with comrade best.

                              [Finn and Poe embrace.

---

[29] *Editor's translation:* The medal once awarded to brave Han—
Hard won for courage in the battle long
Ago, for which I once was overlook'd—
Now given unto me by kindly Maz.
Keen am I this memento to receive,
Yet did assume 'twas lost some years ago.
O, decades after swiftly fall the tears
Unbidden but sincerely from mine eyes.
Past all mine expectation is this gift,
E'en as I from this final battle rest.
True kinfolk have I found within this band,
Exciting ventures making my soul bright—
Replete this Wookiee's spirit is with light.

Enter REY, *landing and emerging from the X-wing.*
She disembarks, spots BB-8, *and runs to him.*

REY   Thou tender droid, I'll thine antenna check.
               I could not fail this mission, dost thou see—
               What wouldst thou do sans me to straighten it?   30
BB-8   Zzwa flibrooh roilzoom fllizooz blisflit blis!
                              [Jannah approaches Lando.
JANNAH   I prithee, General, whence comest thou?
LANDO   Gold system. What of thee, kid? Whence com'st thou?
JANNAH   Nay, I know not.
LANDO   —Belike we shall find out.
                         [Finn and Poe spot Rey and approach
                              her. They all embrace.
REY   We three at long last reunited are.   35
POE   We three, the blessèd words ring as a knell.
FINN   We three who e'er have fought and lov'd as one.
REY   Here let the story rest, the battles cease,
               Here is the glad conclusion of our tale,
               Here friends and comrades are elated, and   40
               Here shall they mourn for all whom they did lose.
POE   Ye watchers all, amid the earnest woes
               That crowd around our path, which turn e'en now
               To gladness, hear this message we relay:
               Hope is the spark that ye should ne'er forsake.   45
FINN   Our story finishes, but yours endures.
               Resistance is the pathway of the just.
               Our star wars, now, are ended, for the nonce—
               Have they mov'd ye to meaningful response?
                         [All freeze as Rey takes center stage.
REY   Flew I, thereafter, in the *Falcon* fast,   50

Obtaining Tatooine's bleak fields at last.
Resolving to perform a final deed,
By way of Luke's old home did I proceed.
Eventually, I came to the place,
Near unaffected by time's steady pace.   55
Applying nimble, scavenger-like skill,
Next I slid down a gentle, sandy hill,
Descending to the home where Luke once grew—
I sens'd, therein, his presence through and through.
The lightsabers I carried in my care—   60
One Leia's, which she later did forswear,
One Luke's, with which he fought the Empire strong—
Now I wrapp'd in a cloth I'd brought along.
Entrusting all their power to the land,
Sand, by the Force, engulf'd them as I'd plann'd.   65
Hereafter they shall rest from all their toil,
Amidst a hidden vault of sandy soil.

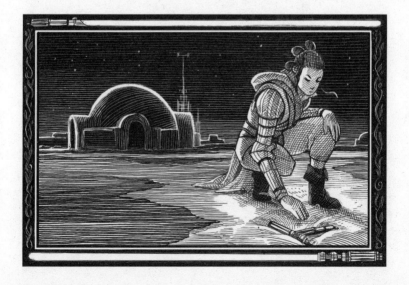

Revealing my new lightsaber of gold,
Excited, once more, to my friends behold,
Declaring my work done on Tatooine,   70
Arose I with a most contented mien.
In mine own thoughts consumèd, by and by,
Met I a woman as she wander'd nigh.
Anon she ask'd my name while passing through.
Rey was mine answer till she ask'd, "Rey who?"   75
Emerg'd then Luke and Leia, wondrous pair,
Delivering mine answer o'er the air:
Rey Skywalker. Yea, thus shall I be known,
Asserting that their fam'ly is mine own.
With hope I look'd toward the double sun,   80
Now mindful that my tale had just begun.

                                        [Exeunt omnes.

END.

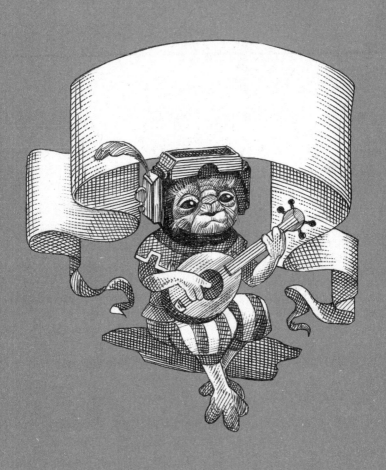

AFTERWORD.

How fortunate we are to live in a time when *Star Wars* is experiencing a resurgence in movies, shows, books, comics, theme parks, and more. Like millions of other people, I was looking forward to *The Rise of Skywalker*, watching the trailers but trying to preserve as much mystery as possible. On opening night, I experienced the joy of seeing the movie unfold with various surprises, resolutions, and emotions. I hope you had the same experience. Almost immediately, I was thinking about how to adapt it into Shakespeare's voice.

Many people noticed that the final scene between Rey and Ben is similar to the end of *Romeo and Juliet*; one person appears dead, the other enters and sees them dead, then the first person awakes and the other person dies. My adaptation gives full voice to that parallel, as Rey and Ben borrow lines from Juliet and Romeo (respectively) once Ben enters and sees Rey lifeless. (Of course, edits were required. After all, when the scene is over Rey is still alive—unlike Juliet.)

In 2019, I listened to the audiobook of *William Shakespeare's Star Wars* for the first time in a few years, and I was reminded how strict my iambic pentameter was in my first book. Not only did I adhere to the meter, but I used almost no weak endings (an eleventh syllable at the end of the line). As I started writing *William Shakespeare's The Merry Rise of Skywalker*, I decided to give myself the challenge of stricter iambic pentameter than I've used in years. As a result—not that I expect you to have noticed—there are fewer than ten weak endings in this book.

Because of the characters who appear in *The Rise of Skywalker*, I revisited almost all of the conventions I created in my previous eight books. In case you're keeping track, or in case these conventions are new to you: Rey has some acrostic speeches, Finn uses *f*s and *n*s in every line, Poe borrows from Edgar Allan Poe in each of his lines, the villains deliver villanelles, R2-D2 addresses the audience in asides, Chewbacca's grunts and growls are "translated," BB-8 uses a skip code, the voice of Yoda has two haiku, Mace Windu references the title of a Samuel L. Jackson movie, Aftab Ackbar inherits his father's -ap endings, and we even get brief lines from Ewoks and porgs.

You'll find Easter eggs throughout the book, as always. These include a tribute to Peter Mayhew, lines borrowed from various well-known authors, and throwbacks to other installments of the William Shakespeare's Star Wars series. As in *William Shakespeare's Jedi the Last*, one Easter egg bears explanation. *The Rise of Skywalker* includes a brief cameo from John Williams, the famous composer of the *Star Wars* score and other well-known cinematic soundtracks. In the movie, he plays a bartender named Oma Tres, who glares at the main characters as they enter his bar (particularly C-3PO, because we all know droids aren't welcome in cantinas). Oma Tres doesn't speak in the movie, but I decided he should have some lines here. More than that, I wanted to write a speech that uniquely captures John Williams's music. I decided to hide the *Star Wars* theme in the speech itself, encoding the melody in the dots above the lowercase *i*s and uppercase O*s to represent music notes on a staff. The dotted *i*s represent eighth notes and the O*s indicate either quarter notes or half notes. Turn the book 90 degrees counterclockwise, and you can see the sheet music come to life. (This is the kind of thing that makes my geek heart very happy.)

Since I have many years bartended here,
Time hath put strange events athwart my path,
Sights never seen have pass'd my watchful eyes.
Here walks——, heav'n!—a band that seemeth base—
The metal knave, he frankleth...the stays,
Were my shrewd rules establish'd presently.
Alas, the central statutes in the bar
Were never set by mine astute decrees.
Thus shall I let them pass me peacef'lly.
Ne'er shall a creature say that mine Tres
Hath ever treated anyone with hate,
Abusèd all the strength his status bears,
And acted aught but kindly ev'ry day.
Nay, I shall serve sans further statement.
Regardless, they that pass near mine Tres
May feel my sneer when walking past the bar,
May sense the deep chagrin where falls my stare,
May grasp resentments and distaste nearby——
If I have hurt them, then mercy grant.

Nine movies—and nine books—later, the Skywalker saga is complete. It has been a privilege to reimagine all nine episodes of the Skywalker story, and I'm honored to have made my small contribution to the stories we all adore. See you around the galaxy, friends.

ACKNOWLEDGMENTS.

This book is dedicated to my parents-in-law, Jeff and Caryl Creswell. To have wonderful in-laws is to be a lucky man indeed.

Thank you to my parents, Bob and Beth Doescher, my brother Erik and sister-in-law Em, and their daughters Aracelli and Addison.

Thank you to Josh Hicks, Alexis Kaushansky, and their daughter Ruby. Thank you to Tom George, Kristin Gordon, Chloe Ackerman, and Graham Steinke. Thank you to Heidi Altman, Chris Martin, Naomi Walcott, and Ethan Youngerman. Collectively, they are the Rey and Poe to my Finn (minus the fan theories of our romance).

Thank you to Murray Biggs, my friend, my former college professor, and a Shakespearean scholar par excellence. While I wrote this book, Murray wrote to me: "Well, aren't you something. Mind you, we always knew that—though there's still some doubt about what that something is, and how much we should have to do with it." I can't think of a more accurate description of what most of my family and friends think of me.

Thank you to the good people of Quirk Books, each one of them a joy: Jhanteigh Kupihea, Nicole De Jackmo, Rebecca Gyllenhaal, Brett Cohen, Christina Tatulli, Kelsey Hoffman, Jane Morley, Andie Reid, Ryan Hayes, Megan DiPasquale, and the rest of the team. Thank you to Nicholas Delort for illustrating all nine of these Shakespeare's Star Wars books.

Thank you to friends and family near and far: Audu Besmer, Jane Bidwell, Travis Boeh and Sarah Woodburn, Chris Buehler and Marian Hammond, Erin and Nathan Buehler, Melody and Jason Burton, Cate and Josiah Carminati, Antwon Chavis and Nate Housel, Joel Creswell, Sibyl Siegfried, Sophie, and Caroline, Katherine Creswell and Spencer Nietmann, Jen Echternach, Jeanette Ehmke, Holly

Havens, Mona and Roland Havens, Jim and Nancy Hicks, Anne Huebsch, Apricot, David, Isaiah and Oak Irving, Jerryn Johnston, Rebecca Lessem, Lisa Lomax, Andrea Martin, Sierra Maxwell, Bruce McDonald, Joan and Grady Miller, Tara and Michael Morrill, Lucy and Tim Neary, Bill Rauch, Scott Roehm, Helga, Michael, and Isabella Scott, Susan Scharfman, J. and K. Thomas, Ryan, Nicole, Mackinzie, Audrey and Lily Warne-McGraw, Steve Weeks, Eva Williams, Ben and Katie Wire, and Dan Zehr.

Thank you to the 4,000-plus members of the Shakespeare 2020 Project, who are reading through the complete works of the Bard this year. It's more fun—and a much larger group—than I imagined possible.

Thank you to my spouse Jennifer, heart of my heart, who after nearly twenty years is still the person I choose every day. Thank you to my sons Liam and Graham, who got me to download Snapchat.

William Shakespeare's
Star Wars: Verily, A New Hope

William Shakespeare's
The Empire Striketh Back

COLLECT THE

William Shakespeare's
The Jedi Doth Return

William Shakespeare's
The Phantom of Menace

William Shakespeare's
The Clone Army Attacketh

William Shakespeare's
Tragedy of the Sith's Revenge

ENTIRE SAGA!

William Shakespeare's
Force Doth Awaken

William Shakespeare's
Jedi the Last

SONNET 9

The hurly-burly's done, the web is won . . .

The battle o'er, the villain vanquish'd quite,
Rey, Finn, and Poe now lead a merry band,
Good hath prevail'd, the wrong hath come out right—
Our heroes rest in celebration grand.
With smile upon your face, your browser ope
And hie unto the **Quirk Books website** soon.
There shalt thou put within thine eyeballs' scope
Frivolity throughout the website strewn.
A **teachers guide** is gratis on the site,
With which thou shalt learn more about the book.
An **interview with Ian Doescher** might
Be just what thou dersir'st: a closer look.
All this and more find thou with much aplomb,
When thou dost get thee to quirkbooks.com.

www.quirkbooks.com/merryriseofskywalker